Eating Women, Telling Tales

Zubaan was set up in 2003 as an imprint of Kali for Women, India's first feminist publishing house, whose name is synonymous with women's writing of quality in South Asia. Zubaan has worked to continue and expand on the pioneering list built up by Kali, and many of the books published by us are today considered to be key texts of feminist scholarship.

To mark our tenth anniversary, we are delighted to offer you ten of our classic titles in bold new editions. These are a mixture of original fiction, translations, memoir and non-fiction on a variety of subjects. Each book is unique; each sheds a different light on the world seen through women's eyes, and each holds its place in the world of contemporary women's writing.

Zubaan is proud that these gifted writers have chosen to entrust us with their work, and we are pleased to be able to re-issue these titles to a new readership in the twenty-first century.

Zubaan Classics

Fiction
Temsula Ao *These Hills Called Home*
Kunzang Choden *The Circle of Karma*
Bulbul Sharma, *Eating Women, Telling Tales*
Vandana Singh *The Woman Who Thought She Was a Planet and Other Stories*

Memoir
Baby Halder *A Life Less Ordinary*

Non-fiction
Uma Chakravarti *Rewriting History: The Life and Times of Pandita Ramabai*
Preeti Gill (ed.) *The Peripheral Centre: Voices from the Northeast*
Sharmila Rege *Writing Caste/Writing Gender: Narrating Dalit Women's Testimonios*
Kumkum Sangari and Sudesh Vaid (eds.) *Recasting Women: Essays in Colonial History*
Tanika Sarkar *Words to Win: The Making of a Modern Autobiography*

Note: Since all books are reprints, the bibliographical information they contain on authors has not been updated, and several titles mentioned in them as forthcoming are more than likely to have already appeared.

Eating Women, Telling Tales
Stories about Food

Bulbul Sharma

ZUBAAN
an imprint of Kali for Women
128 B Shahpur Jat, 1st floor
NEW DELHI 110 049
Email: contact@zubaanbooks.com
Website: www.zubaanbooks.com

First published by Zubaan 2009

10 9 8 7 6 5 4 3 2

ISBN   978 93 81017 89 0

Zubaan is an independent feminist publishing house based in New Delhi with a strong academic and general list. It was set up as an imprint of India's first feminist publishing house, Kali for Women, and carries forward Kali's tradition of publishing world quality books to high editorial and production standards. *Zubaan* means tongue, voice, language, speech in Hindustani. Zubaan is a non-profit publisher, working in the areas of the humanities, social sciences, as well as in fiction, general non-fiction, and books for children and young adults under its Young Zubaan imprint.

Typeset by Jojy Philip, New Delhi 100 015
Printed at Raj Press, R-3 Inderpuri, New Delhi 110 012

Eating women, telling tales

The crows sat in a circle waiting for the funeral feast to begin. In their eagerness to get the best leftovers, they had gathered a bit too early. Badibua, the main cook who was to prepare all the favourite dishes of the deceased, Bhanurai Jog, had not yet arrived. She had left for the fish market at dawn along with Hema and the ferry which was to bring them back from the haat across the river, was late as usual. The crows raised their necks and flapped their wings impatiently. From their vantage point on top of the water tank on the roof they had a clear view of the road and could see all the people as they got down from tongas, carts or the boat and walked into the house where the funeral feast was to be held.... It was around six in morning, a light breeze ruffled their feathers as the birds waited and watched....

So far only Malarani had arrived in a rickshaw, a huge pumpkin in her lap. A little later, just when the crows were wondering whether to fly down to the market or look around for another home to stalk, the ferry arrived and Badibua stumbled out ahead of all the other passengers. Behind her, almost hidden by her vast girth, shuffled Hema her young servant woman, carrying a covered basket. The crows gave a squawk of delight. They knew there was a whole fish in that basket, head, entrails and tail intact. They shuffled a bit to show their excitement taking care not to lose their places on the edge of the water tank.

Then, in quick succession, the other women arrived. A rickshaw ringing its bell loudly brought Shashi, her short hair flying in the breeze. She was followed by the two twin sisters Nanni and Sharada who came in a tonga. Then the crows, on high alert now, saw Choni emerge from another tonga along with a servant boy carrying a basket of vegetables. She argued with the tonga driver about the fare and then finally settled it with an angry shrug. She walked ahead as the servant boy trailed behind balancing the basket on his head. "Hurry, why are you walking like a girl, come on now ... we don't have all day," she shouted turning around, and the boy smiled at her from the shadow of the basket perched on his head.

Dark green bitter gourd, bottle shaped gourd, cauliflower, fresh spinach, red chaulai, flat beans, and a dozen big round eggplants jostled as the boy tried to walk faster. All these were vegetables the late Shri Bhanurai Jog loved and had to be cooked on his death anniversary feast today. The women were not sure whether he liked eggplant, most men did not, calling it a vegetable without any "gun" or merit but the women loved thick slices of aubergines deep fried in mustard oil, so they decided to include the humble eggplant. The menu, like every year, had been decided by Badibua since she was the eldest surviving relative of the dead man. There was, of course, his son who lived abroad but none spoke about him. They remembered that he had not even come for the funeral. They remembered his wife, a shy gentle creature who had died a few years before him.

Year before last an old aunt of Bhanurai Jog, Shantirani, who claimed to be a hundred, had done the main dish but she had become a bit senile, and very unpredictable. At first she had cooked happily with them, regaling them with endless stories about her late husband and his various love affairs, then suddenly she got up to chase the guests with a broom, screaming at them, "Come to steal my gold bangles, I will kill you, thieves, dogs." They had to tie her up with a saree and calm her down with fennel juice. Now she could no longer be safely included in the cooking of the funeral feast and it was decided earlier this year to install Badibua as the main cook.

There were eight of them this morning chosen by Badibua. All the women were related, some closely and some so distant that only the very old aunts could remember the connection. There were other women in the late Bhanurai Jog's vast family who could have qualified to cook today but the old man had cut off connections with them for years. They came for the funeral though just to see who had been left his vast property and now they were not on speaking terms with Badibua ever since they found out it was she who had inherited the house and all the land surrounding it. Overnight from being a poor relative whom everyone was fond of, she became a much envied woman whom they loved to criticise. "So distantly related yet she gets it all."

Badibua did not care and enjoyed her new found wealth happily, filling the old house with the few members of the family she liked and her old friends. Though she still could not understand why Bhanurai Jog, such a dried up old man who everyone had been scared of, had called her one day and told her she was to have the house. Maybe because she had been a childhood friend of his wife's, though they'd been out of touch for years.

The women quickly touched Badibua's feet and then, tucking their sarees around their waists, they sat down in a circle around a huge pile of vegetables. A servant brought a brass plate with eight knives and placed them in front of Badibua respectfully as if it was an offering to the gods. Badibua shrugged her shoulders, it was an old habit of hers and she did it every few minutes as if getting rid of something on her back, and looked around. The women waited to see who she would choose to cut the important vegetables today. It would decide how the morning would go. Badibua nodded her head at Malarani and everyone sighed with relief. That had always been the pattern of cooking the annual funeral feast, the pumpkin whould be cut by the senior-most woman and Badibua had not wavered. She and Malarani would lead the vegetable cutters. If she had chosen one of the younger women, like Shashi or Choni newly inducted into the group, there would have been grumblings and the cooking would taste bitter. Badibua as usual had chosen the right woman to be her commander-in-chief. The younger two could learn from them.

They quickly began cleaning the vegetables in a large bucket of water. The servants had washed them before bringing them to the circle but they could never be trusted to do it properly.

The two chosen women began to slice the pumpkin, Malarani worked with great speed and fineness but she took care not to be faster than Badibua because that would look bad and the women would think her shameless. They all knew she could cut vegetables faster than anyone else in the group but there was no need to show off. The red cement floor was soon slippery with water, discarded spinach leaves and stems of eggplants.

The seven women gathered around the vegetables could have easily been sisters. They all had the same clear golden skin, all except Shashi who was so pale she could be called Kashmiri. They all had round faces with fine eyebrows. slightly pointed noses and thick black hair. Only Shashi had cut her hair recently when she'd gone to Delhi for a friend's wedding. In their family she was the first one to do so and though Badibua was not happy with her niece's short hair, she did not say anything. She was very fond of this lively girl whose mother had died just after giving birth to her. Badibua could see her dead sister's cheerful face laughing at her when she looked at Shashi. She shifted her huge girth and pushed the pumpkin pieces to one side. "You look like a boy, you do" said Choni, who was always a bit nasty to her. "This year the coriander and mint we grew is really good. You can smell the fragrance even before you begin to grind it" said Malarani, her fingers sorting out the wilted ones from the bunch of fresh coriander leaves. She looked up and smiled at Choni who scowled back, "You know, I love growing things. Maybe I was a mali in my last life," she said, laughing.

Badibua felt a surge of affection for her cousin, her mother's sister's daughter. Life had treated her so harshly, no husband, no children, yet she was always so happy. "You couldn't have with those pretty, plump hands," Shashi said giving her aunt a hug. Choni threw the potato she was peeling into a cauldron of water and said, "You could be a mali even now, masi. Might earn you some money instead of asking for charity." She gave her aunt a sideways glance. "She never asks for charity, Choni, I think you are being very rude to masi," said Shashi. Malarani laughed and ruffled Shashi's hair. She did not mind Choni's words. What did it matter what anyone said? There were so many things in life that did not matter to her anymore and she often thought about them and felt happy. She threw out a coriander stem. One of the waiting crows flew down to examine it and then flew away. It had lost its place on the water tank now and gave a harsh cry. "I remember how my mother-in-law used to make this chutney. She gave it to us when we were young. The old witch is dead now. Do not speak evil of the dead they say, but there is not one good thing I can say about that woman," said Malarani shaking her head. "That is very rare for you," said Badibua. "I cannot forget what she did to that poor girl. Remember her, that sweet girl who my youngest brother-in-law married, you know the one who went to work in England…"

The women knew a story was coming and settled down to listen. They spread their bodies in a more comfortable position, but their hands continued to chop and clean. It was the first story of the morning and they hoped it was not a sad one. Later on there would be sad ones, sweet ones, bitter ones and angry ones as each woman would tell her tale. Five stories while cutting the vegetables, one while cleaning the rice husk and maybe two while stirring the kheer. Sometimes there was time for a few more after lunch when the rest of house was asleep. No one could be sure how many stories a day would give.

One

The fragrance of sweet basil filled her heart with sadness. She crushed each leaf tenderly, holding the stem between her thumb and forefinger so that it would not feel the pain. She whispered a few words, the same words she used when she caressed her husband after they had made love. Maya had all day to prepare the basil, mango, ginger and coriander chutney her mother-in-law had asked her to make today. "It is only for you, girl, so make just one katoriful" the old lady has told her, her eyes squinting in the bright sunlight. Maya had to pluck the leaves herself each morning after she'd had a bath and said her prayers. The patch of herbs was in a secluded spot just below their house but she had to go all the way round, skirting the entire verandah because her father-in-law and his two friends sat there playing chess. When she had first arrived as a young bride in this house which rose like a citadel of spun sugar in the midst of a pine forest, Maya did not know the rules of the house. She walked right across the old men playing chess, folded her hands in a quick greeting, pointed out a honey-bee which was hovering around her father-in-law's gaping mouth before hurrying past to the garden. When she returned, the bundle of herbs tied in her saree palla, her arms full of aubergines still damp with dew drops, green translucent peas, one half-opened cauliflower and a tiny bouquet of red chillies tucked into her waist, a strange silence greeted her.

"Come in, girl, leave the vegetables outside," her mother-in-law said in a sharp voice which made the pale morning light tremble. Maybe she should not have plucked the vegetables as yet, perhaps they were not yet ready. She should have waited till the aubergines had weighed their stems down to touch the earth and the cauliflower had a full circle of creamy white florets. That squinty-eyed gardener must have complained to the old lady. "What were you doing. You shameless girl! Are you mad? Don't ever walk like that past the men with your face uncovered. Have you no sense? What did your mother teach you, girl? Oh, what a day! The entire village will now gossip about this shameful act of yours!" said her mother-in-law, rubbing her fists over her eyes, forcing the tears out of her glittering-with-malice eyes. "Go. Stay indoors till we ask for you…Go now…I feel sick looking at your hussy face." The old lady said all this picking up a handful of fine betel nuts she had been cutting while she screamed at Maya. Her hand missed her mouth and the betel nut slices, as fragile as bits of parchment, fell down her blouse, settling down like old scars in her deep bosom. Maya laughed out loudly and then slowly walked into her room, tying a languid knot in her long hair.

"We have to do something about her, are you listening?" said Gitasri to her husband who was half reclining on the bed, resting on three fat pillows embroidered with pink daisies, tucked under his head which made his chin sink into his chest. He looked like a cherub nestling amongst flowers. Gitasri looked at him with irritation. Was he a grown man with four sons or a silly young boy clutching his pillow all day? She wished she had married the dark boy her mother had suggested. Dark men are real men, the blood in their veins is thick and warm, her mother always said though her own husband, Gitasri's beloved Baba, was as fair as an Englishman. "Yes...yes..." her pink-cheeked husband muttered dreamily as he recalled the chess move he had made this morning. How stunned Bosebabu had been when he moved his bishop forward at that precise moment. His wife suddenly pulled out one of the pillows, disturbing the cosy nest of perfect balance he had achieved after so much effort. He sighed and looked at her. The betel nut had streaked her lips dark brown and for the first time in the forty years that he had been married to her, he noticed how sharp and pointed her teeth were. "I always knew we had chosen the wrong one. Did you notice how she looked around the room at each one of us, not once did she cast her eyes down modestly like a new bride should during the ceremony. When I stared at her she did not look away but continued to stare back at me with those glittering eyes. First I thought the fire from the havan had touched her eyes but no it was not that. Now I can see...something strange in her eyes. They flash like cat's eyes."

"I tell you, are you listening to me.... Are you? I feel like strangling you with this flower bedecked pillow of yours. Listen, carefully. I tell you it will bring disaster one day to our house. The way she holds her head, raising her neck high, laughs in that mocking way when I give her instructions about something...I tell you, it frightens me. So much arrogance is not good in a woman, who knows what she may do one day. I worry about my poor son...so gentle..." said Gitasri and her husband replied with a gentle snore. Gitasri looked down at him, pulled one pillow out and threw it on the floor.... Wretched daisy flowers. I hope they choke him to death.

She had to speak to Bhagwan. He would tell her what to do. All her four daughter-in-laws were so gentle, docile with forever downcast eyes and hunched shoulders. Even that barren cow Malarani. She did not even mind when Gitasri kicked her, she just smiled like an imbecile. She smiled even when they got another wife to replace her. Wretched woman turned out to be barren too! No, only this Maya, curse her, walked around the house like a lioness with cubs. She was too proud because of her beautiful face and her long hair which swung below her hips. "Do not bring a beauty," her mother had advised her and she had chosen simple, plain brides with broad hips and healthy teeth for the other three sons. Good well behaved girls, docile, obedient and good breeders. Each one, except Malarani, had produced a son within the first year of their marriage and now they spent all their time in the kitchen supervising the servants. Of course they asked her permission for everything: what to cook, what saree or piece of jewellery to wear, which fast to keep and how often. She also rationed how much time they could spend talking to their husbands and made sure the doors to their bedrooms were always open. She could walk in any time she liked.

Gitasri considered herself a fair woman so she let them manage their children's and their husbands' day-to-day life, like which kurta to wear, whether to grow a moustache or not. But she and only she took the final decisions on important matters like what to name the children, how much money to give to the sons and how often they could visit their wives at night. She knew they would never step outside the line she had drawn for them, but run around, and play happily within the circle like her grandsons' pet white mice on their toy wheels. She never had to worry even for a day about her older sons and their steady, cow wives. But Subir, her youngest, who had been born when she had almost reached menopause and thought her womb had dried up, was different from the other boys right from childhood. She loved him most of all and let him do whatever he wanted. But that was the mistake she made. He ran out too far and now she could not hold him down anymore. He wanted to see his bride. "See his own bride before the wedding? Are we blind or what? Too much studying leads to this," her relatives had said, their faces full of spite. Subir was the first one in the family to finish college and as if that was not enough, he won a scholarship and went off to the London School of Economics to study further. "What is the need for all this book learning?" she said but he would not listen.

Now to make matters worse he had got a job there in that foreign land. Gitasri had warned her husband not to send him but like all her warnings this one too flew past his ears like a buzzing fly. Chess, chess and more chess was all he thought about. That and his daisy pillow. "Let him see his bride. What is the harm? Educated boys like to make their own choice." So Subir came to India for a week, saw Maya and chose her at once though they had lined up five more girls for him. Maya, the only daughter of wealthy landowning family, had finished school and could recite English poetry as well as Bengali. She brought with her a huge dowry which helped to settle the debts her husband had got into when the timber prices crashed and the money was enough to also pay for their younger daughter's wedding. "Good luck for us that Subir chose this one and not that plump one with the miser father who sent us only one basket of fruit with his daughter's black and white photograph to hide the fact that she was coal black. Our Subir picked the right one in one second. See, all this English education does help." Her husband had said, stroking the diamond ring Maya's father had given him as a gift along with an ivory chess set.

Gitasri watched her sleeping husband for a while, her anger melting away. It was hard to feel angry with him for too long.

Her silly boy-husband, his double chin tucked onto his chest, his tiny ears and long lashed eyelids drooping with slumber filled her with irritation and love. She picked up the daisy pillow from the floor and placed it next to him and went out.

The crows called outside the window and somewhere far away in the forest other birds echoed their harsh calls with sweet songs. Dawn broke over the forest with a sudden stream of light, though the moon, faded but full and round, was still high up in the sky. Bhagwan should be in his ashram, fasting for 'kartik purnima' which was tomorrow. She would go to him today, take Maya with her. He would tell her what to do. He would tell her how to break the girl in before it was too late. She should have taken Maya to him a long time ago but how was she to know that the wretched girl would have so much spirit in her. Yes, Bhagwan would show her the right way to mellow this girl.

Maya got out of bed as soon as she heard the crows call. Outside her window the roses spread their scent trap calling all the insects to them greedily. Today she would write another letter, telling him about the insect she had found in the cabbage patch. "It was green with brown edges. It was shaped just like a tender corn cob, " Maya composed the words in her mind She would have to look up the spelling of 'edges' and 'tender'. Subir wrote such long letters with so many difficult words but she managed to understand them without looking at the dictionary. She could picture herself in his room which was next to a train station. But this was not a regular train but one that ran under the earth taking the people from one part of the city to the next. Maya had been to Calcutta once with her mother to buy sarees for her wedding and she had seen how people scurried from one end of the city to another. But in London they could not be seen at all because they all travelled hidden deep in the belly of the earth.

"When you come here, we will go around the city in red double decker buses. You can see everything from the top window of the bus." Subir described all the places they would visit once she got her passport and went to London to live with him. "Speak in English as much as you can so that you can understand what these people say. They are kind and helpful but they speak very fast sometimes swallowing their words. I had a lot of difficulty when I first came here," wrote Subir in his clear, rounded hand, the blue ink making small smudges around all the 'o's. Maya read his letters over and over again and now she knew the names of all the places they would see, walking everywhere together or sitting in the red buses with big windows. Buckingham Palace where the Queen lived with her husband who was not the King. Big Ben which was a big clock that could be heard all over the city like a temple bell, Tower of London which was a fort where the Queen of London kept her jewels. They were guarded day and night by her special guards who wore fur hats so that their ears would not get cold at night.

Maya had knitted five pullovers for Subir and two for herself from wool her father had sent her from home. She looked at the sunshine playing on the courtyard stones and wished she could go home for a few days. But no one would let her. In this house they all lived by rules her mother-in-law had made for them. The other daughters-in-law obeyed her because they did not want their husbands to scold them but Maya was not afraid. She would ask today if she could go home for the pooja which her mother was planning to do soon for her brother's first son. All her cousins would be there and they could roam the entire plantation on the horse buggy that her brothers could drive like warriors of old. The mango trees would be full of green fruit and the guavas too would be ready. Yes, I will ask her today after I have made the basil, mango, ginger chutney. Why does she keep feeding me these strange things as if I am a goat? I think she dislikes me. I don't care. If she thinks I am going to lick her feet like the other girls, she is mistaken. Only Malarani, the middle daughter-in-law was kind to her. Poor woman, she was barren and her husband had married again and soon she would have to go back to her father's house. The old woman had announced it yesterday and no one had protested "She has a box full of gold coins. Every Diwali she gives us one coin. Those of us she is really pleased with she sometimes even gives two," her elder sister-in-law had said the other day. Maya did not want a gold coin. Her husband earned enough for her. What would they do in London with gold coins? Give them to the Queen she thought and laughed.

The rickshaw swayed at every turn making Maya fall against her mother-in-law's plump shoulders. She smelt of sandalwood and rose water. Maya had been told to cover her face but she kept the sari palla pulled to one side so that she could look out at the fields. The path rose gently skirting the rocky hills and then suddenly diving low to run through the grassy meadows. Butterflies with yellow and orange wings sat briefly on the handle of the cycle, fluttering their wings restlessly and then flew away slowly as if tired of this movement. A soft warm breeze touched their faces, making the sweat on her mother-in-law's cheeks dry in silvery patches. "You will bow your head at Bhagwan's feet. There will be a bowl of water – dip your hair and then wash his feet with the tips. Do not put too much water. It is always chilly in the ashram and he might catch a cold. He is very fragile now at his age though once he was such a strapping young man. Strode everywhere like a lion. His followers could not keep up with him and had to run, poor creatures," said Gitasri smiling and suddenly Maya felt a surge of affection for her. She wanted to put her arms around her but knew the old lady hated being touched by anyone. Even the grandchildren kept their distance except to touch her feet every morning. They never jumped on her lap like her brother's children did at home, squeezing their grandmother's arms and jutting their heads into her lap like goats.

Kadam, jamun and mango trees began to shade their path and the stones, lined along the path, had vermilion marks on them to show the way to the ashram. Saffron, white and orange flags floated from the topmost branches of the trees, some were spotted with pigeon droppings. Maya lifted her pallav to look at an old peepal tree which was covered with bits of red cloth, tied around the branches. "People make a wish here, tie a red cloth. They come and untie it when their wish comes true, " said the rickshaw-wallah, turning his head to speak to munshi who was in the rickshaw behind them. Their servants with the baskets of sweets and fruits trailed far behind in a bullock cart. Maya looked back and saw that some of the red cloths were so old that they had faded to white. Maybe people had forgotten to untie them or their wishes had come true too late and they had died. "Do many wishes come true? Do people come back to untie them?" asked Maya but the rickshaw man did not reply. Gitasri coughed angrily and pulled the palla down on Maya's face, her heavy gold bangle caught the silk threads on the saree border and tore it.

"She likes chutney, Bhagwan. Sour things – eats them all the time," said Gitasri softly, pressing Bhagwan's feet. "She is not with child as yet." Maya had been sent to gather guavas from the tree which grew in the courtyard. Bhagwan allowed only women to pluck the fruit because "their touch makes the tree more fertile," he said. But only young, married women, not widows or barren ones. Those were the ones with tainted hands, cursed by the gods, discarded by men. The tree would stop giving fruit if women like that touched even a leaf. Maya was exactly the kind of woman he liked. Young, with flesh firm on her body, sparkling eyes and glossy hair. Teeth like pearls and breath scented with musk. But ever since he had taken his vows he had had to keep them far away and only tend to these dried up old hags who sat at his feet all day long. Their faded, sad eyes adoring him and white hair, which smelt of old age, bowing at his feet, gnarled hands tugging at his body. Maya was a ripe, forbidden fruit which he would love to suck, maybe in another lifetime. "See how she walks, Bhagwansree, not at all the way a well brought up girl from a good family should. How she got to be like this I don't know. Her mother is a godfearing woman, prays and fasts all through the year. Could be her father or her five brothers who have made her like this." Gitasri droned on as Omprabhu Dayal, who liked being called Bhagwan by his disciples though he always made a mild protest when they did that, watched Maya through half-shut eyes. He would enjoy taming her. Jaggery, fennel, pregnant cow's urine, fenugreek and ash from the funeral pyre of a pious woman whose husband is alive. He would like to keep her here for a few days but he knew that was not possible. Gitasri would not allow it. She wanted to break her spirit but not lose her altogether. That English-educated son of her's would attack her. The girl was going to live with him soon in a foreign land but still Gitasri wanted to teach her to be docile. "For my son's sake. For the future. Or else she'll become too set in her shameless ways." Omprabhu nodded. "You cannot teach an old cow the tender moo of a calf," he said yawning. He could break her in one night like he had done so many other women. Holding their neck in one hand while he shoved his erect manhood into them. Sometimes he had to cover their mouths but most of the time they had fainted by the time he came near them. Ripe poppy seeds pounded with green chillies and ginger made their body pliant and they began to float as soon as the sharp taste touched their tongues. Some were not even aware that he had penetrated them though they bled for quite a while later. Their families took them back and when the child, always a son, was born, (God was kind to him) they sent him gift of fruits, clothes, sweets and silver coins. He never saw the women again, never looked at his sons. But now he had taken his vows. If only this one had come a few months ago. He was not sure of his powers anymore. Still he would try. No harm in that.

Maya came back cradling an armful of guavas in her sari palla. She took a green one out, polished it, and then bit hard into it, looking straight into his eyes. Omprabhu was startled by her direct gaze, none of the women had ever dared to look at him like this. He suddenly felt nervous and had to look down at his feet. A tremor of irritation ran through his body and he wanted to slap the girl. Gitasri was right, they had to do something before it was too late and the girl had learnt to walk too proud and tall.

Jaggery, black basil, neem, goat's milk and poppy seeds ground with sesame oil. A few bits of alum and then the shaving of silver that had aged under the soil for a hundred years —that was enough for most women but Maya was different. He would have to think of something stronger for her, she was like the mare that was brought to him last year. He had tried everything but she continued to kick and flare her nostrils. Then he found this powder in the loft where his master had hidden his prized herbs. Black pearls from China, turquoise from Tibet and a huge rare blood coral from Ladakh, mixed with the urine of a civet cat.

"Use these precious stones with care, my son. Weigh each gram before you give them to anyone, especially women. They travel down their bloodstream very fast, twisting their veins, sometimes driving them insane. Mix them with silver or crushed alum to warm up the blood of frigid women." But he did not want the girl to feel any warmth. He had to make her body hollow, drain her red blood out and fill her veins with crushed pearls and snake venom which had been soaked in opium juice. Then this old coral which lay in his palm like a piece of dried flesh would make the girl sink to the ground like a wilted leaf. He would have liked to taste her before her fires were put out but he could not take the risk even if he had not taken the vows.

He would start the first dose at night and within a week she would be as gentle as a cow – a perfect woman like the gods had ordained her to be – a jewel of a woman to possess, beautiful and pliant. Quiet, docile, soft-spoken, always good tempered, always ready to obey. She would lie softly under her husband receiving his seed, lower her eyes before her elders, cook, clean, tend to their welfare without pause and every month on full moon nights, wash his feet with her hair. Her eyes would lose their shine yet be pretty, her skin would be fairer, her hair would grow even more black and glossy, her head, so proud now, would bend as delicately as a lotus bud, ready to bow to everyone's wishes.

"Put your right palm out, girl, take this prasad from Bhagwansree. It will help you get well," said her mother-in-law. Maya wanted to say she was not sick but somehow she could not speak. She felt so sleepy today. The fresh air had made her head heavy and the milk they gave her to drink, laced with spices, was too sweet and creamy. When she touched her forehead her fingers felt cold on her skin. Maybe she was ill – like the old lady said – with some dangerous disease she thought, feeling afraid for the first time in her life. She raised her head to the sky.... She felt she was watching herself from high above.

They left the ashram next day at dawn. Omprabhu did not come out of his room, but Ma went to the door and touched his feet which he stuck out clumsily, his face covered with a white muslin cloth.

Suddenly Maya saw his dead body lying on the floor of the courtyard, surrounded by weeping women.

"Bhagwan will leave us soon" she muttered to Ma when they sat in the rickshaw but the old lady did not hear her. She sat counting her prayer beads all the way home and when they got down from the rickshaw, she did not look at Maya. That was the last time Maya saw daylight.

She went straight to her room and lay down on her bed.

Each morning when she ground the spices with the red powder Bhagwan had given her, her heart bled. Why was she drinking this foul tasting liquid? She did not know. But she had to have it. Her body longed for it and her hands began to tremble if she waited too long for this fiery liquid.

Her long hair began to grow wild and thick and her eyes began to change colour. The maidservant who came to help her bathe was the first one to notice the marks on her body. "They are like holes... As if someone had pressed their fingers into her skin till it bled," she said, her eyes round with horror as she told the other servants though Gitasri had warned her not to talk to anyone about Maya.

Maya never left her room. She lay on the bed talking to herself. Subir's letters lay piled up next to her pillow but though she looked at them all the time, turning the white envelopes in her fingers, smelling their strange foreign smell, she did not read them anymore. She could not remember who Subir was.

Maya's body was pale as the sheets now and when Gitasri entered her room, a sweet aroma of burnt poppy seeds hit her. Maya was half asleep but she sat up and looked at her with glazed eyes.

"Ma, Someone you love is dead.... I can see him on his deathbed, now. Look, there you are beating your breast, you are sitting by the pyre. Cry Ma...I can hear you crying..." Maya said, her voice slurred, her eyes gleaming though her face was puffed up.

Gitasri ran out of the room, covering her mouth with her hand to stop screaming. She leaned against the wall, feeling dizzy and called one of the maids. "Go, at once, to the men's sitting room. Call your master, now. Even if there are visitors tell him to come at once," she said shaking the frightened girl's shoulders and making her cringe at her touch.

When she heard her husband's footsteps outside the room she quickly covered Maya with a sheet and went out to meet him. For some reason she did not want him to inhale this sweet, stale fragrance which flowed from the girl's body. "Will you send someone to my father's house please? I've had a bad premonition." Her husband took her hand and made her sit down. "I was just coming to you. I have some bad news. Bhagwan is no more. They sent word from the ashram just now. He was found dead in the attic, the roof had fallen on him and they had to dig him out. We must prepare to go at once for the funeral."

Maya sang, caressing her hair which now spread out like a river on the floor. She sang bowing her head low, her faded silver eyes now gentle and dead, she sang till it was dark and then she fell asleep.

Two

The women were quiet for a while, the fragrance of coriander and ginger making them think of Maya's fate. Some thought you could not afford to be too proud if you were born a woman, others felt it was important to hold your head high and not let people trample all over you. Maya had done no wrong, she'd just been less docile than the others. Malarani laughed. "I was the most docile one, never lifted my veil, not even to see my husband's face. I was fortunate that they did not take me to that man they called Bhagwan. My mother-in-law thought I was not worth bothering about. 'There is nothing in her womb at all, even Bhagwansree cannot help her,' she said to everyone. So they left me alone. Forgot all about me. I don't know whose fate was better, Maya's or mine," said Malarani and then she shook her head and laughed again.

The other women did not know what to say to her, they looked down and began breaking the spinach leaves quickly. Then Badibua cleared her throat. Another story was coming. They hoped she would tell them the story about her friend Jamini. They had heard this story before yet they were happy to hear about Badibua's friend's son who came after ten years from America to visit his mother. It always broke their hearts, this story. "A mother has every right to love her child in every way she thinks is right," said Badibua, wiping her hands on the edge of her sari.

BADIBUA'S FRIEND JAMINI'S STORY

The dust had settled deep into the crevices and Jamini had to wrap a cloth around a toothbrush to clean it out. Babu had taught her how to do it when he was just ten years old. She was dusting in that half-hearted way just to show Kamala, the girl who came to sweep and swab every morning, that she was not totally disinterested in cleaning the house, but when she came to the terracotta leaves along the edge of the window, she ignored the dark lines of dust that etched their edges. "Ma you forgot the dust...there look...the edges of the leaves," said Babu, lying on the bed with a comic book which had a girl's mutilated body draped on an ape's lap on the cover. Jamini quite liked the dark lines the dust had made on the terracota leaves, giving them an antiquated look so she pretended not to hear. "Ma, the leaves. Wrap a cloth around a toothbrush. I will show you how to do it," Babu said sitting up in the bed. Kamala, impressed with this suggestion, ran to get an old toothbrush from the bathroom. Together they cleaned each leaf, digging out the dust viciously as if it was something living and dangerous which needed to be killed while Jamini stood and watched.

Now, so many years later, she was trying to do the same thing and it was not working. Maybe she was not using enough force. The dust had become a part of the warm red terracota now and Jamini could not see the dark lines anymore as she ran the toothbrush blindly around the edges. "He won't notice all this, leave it now. You know your back will start hurting if you bend so much," Manish said. But Jamini knew her son would notice the leaves as he would notice the faded carpet, the newly repaired sofa covers, the old stone floor and the new set of kitchen knives as soon as he walked into the house, the smell of the foreign land still fresh on his skin... He would laugh at her, hold her hand as they walked around the house, teasing her about her grey hair but his eyes would sweep over the house, checking each thing that offended his fastidious taste, picking out hidden faults with a sudden narrowing of his eyes.

There were only five days left before Babu arrived and the two bedrooms upstairs were still not done. Kamala was still with them after sixteen years and though they had to put up with her mercurial moods, they were lucky to have her. The old house needed so much care and if Babu had not sent them money each month from America, they would not be able to live here. They used the dollars to pay the servants and their taxes and to repair the house and whatever was left they banked for Babu. Though Manish never said anything, Jamini knew he hated taking money from his son. Each time the cheque arrived, usually towards the end of the month, her husband would let the glossy envelope lie on the dining table till she asked him to take it to the bank. He would make excuses and then finally, when Jamini threatened to go herself, he would take the by now curry stained envelope to be cashed. Without a word he would hand her the money, heavy bundles of crisp notes and then shut himself in his study. The next day he would be his normal cheerful self but Jamini had to be careful and never mention Babu's dollars and carry on pretending that they lived on Manish's meagre pension.

Today she would finish the front room and the guest bathroom and then finally start on Babu's room. All through the year no one used this room which Babu had decorated himself, chosing the furniture from an expensive new shop she would never dare to enter, buying complicated electric lights which Jamini had only seen in glossy magazines. This room sat in the middle of the shabby old house like a gleaming jewel and once a week Kamala, who admired Babu more than ever now that she knew somehow that he paid her salary, dusted it carefully with a new duster she kept only for this room. The rest of the house she cleaned half-heartedly with a dirty yellow cloth which had once been Manish's kurta. Every ten days or so she tied a handkerchief around her face and sprayed a green liquid Babu had sent from America called Shine-O. A friend had brought a huge packet with six bottles of this liquid and two sweaters for them a few months ago. The bottle was shaped like a jug and it had a picture of a pretty blonde girl standing near a gleaming glass window. A table with a lamp glittered next to her, and behind her leaves, grass and flowers shone as if touched by a ray of golden light. If they had given the girl two white wings she would have looked just like an angel dancing in heaven. So far they had used only one bottle and when the green liquid finished Jamini could not bear to throw the bottle with the smiling golden girl into the rubbish heap. She had washed it carefully and then filled it with water and planted a long stem of money plant in it. But the leaves turned yellow and died within a week. A strange smell of lime hung in the air for days after Kamala sprayed this green liquid which made Manish sneeze and the lizards too kept out of the room though they roamed the rest of the house freely. "Must have a very American disinfectant along with the polish" said Manish with a low laugh which sounded false. "It keeps us third world humans and lizards out too."

It was raining when Babu's plane landed and Jamini, her hands cold with fear, kept praying that it would not skid on the wet runway. "Ma Durga, bring my son home to me safe.

You have looked after him so well in that faraway land for ten years. Make that plane touch the ground safely, Ma. I will give bhog to you next Tuesday." Jamini kept repeating this under her breath as she watched the plane land through the glass panes of the airport lounge. Suddenly she noticed a pattern of dust on the window panes. "Not my area. Nobody can blame me for this bit of dust," she thought with relief and began praying once more but her mind wandered. Next Tuesday would be fine for the bhog, Ma would not mind waiting till Babu had settled down. His room was sparkling clean, every inch sprayed with the green American disinfectant. The rest of the house shone too, not as brightly as the Shine-O lady's garden but in a quiet faded way. They had bought five cases of mineral water, tomato ketchup, cheese, toilet paper rolls, oats and brown bread as Babu had told them to do in his last letter. She had done everything he had instructed her to do, ticking off the items on the list one by one and now finally they were ready to receive their only son who was coming home after five years! "Look, there he is," said Manish. Jamini straightened her shoulders, moistened her dry lips and went ahead to meet her beloved son. Though she wanted to throw her arms around him and hold him tightly she restrained herself and then suddenly, flooded with a wave of shyness, she just patted his hand.

Babu looked around him, trying not to compare. He had told himself over and over again on the flight home not to be critical. But everything seemed to have deteriorated in the past five years. The streets were more dirty, more noisy and crowded than they had been five years ago, his parents had aged visibly and the house had grown even more shabby than he remembered. His father seem to have lost his memory and kept repeating everything to him as if he was a child and his mother, who used to be such fun, was as quiet as a mouse. Was five years such a long time? Maybe he should have come last year but there was no time. He had just two weeks off after that holiday in Florida. The six weeks he had to stay in India now seemed interminable. "Don't spend all your time in India. Come back after two weeks and we'll go to Alaska. Kate and Mike are taking this fabulous cruise, it'll be such fun," Maria had said. But Babu, who was known as Babs both at work and amongst his friends in New Jersey, thought it would be better if he spent all his time in India, sorting out the house. It was a bore but it had to be done. What a mess everything was in! His father had no idea how to manage anything, yet when anyone tried to advise him, he clamped his lips together and refused to discuss anything. They were sitting, just the two of them, in this huge, rambling house right in the middle of the city with no money to look after the property. It was a golden piece of real estate worth a fortune but his father refused to even think about it. This time he was going to persuade his father to sell the house and move into a smaller flat. It would be so much easier for Ma to look after and he could take some of the money back bit by bit, now that the government allowed it, and pay his mortgage off. But all this would take time and he must spend six weeks here, working on his father who was going to be as obstinate as ever. He only listened to Ma because she always said exactly what he wanted to hear. Babu looked at his mother sitting in the same chair at the dining table as she had always done, the one with a broken leg that shook when you sat down and had to be propped up against the wall. "The old chair has not yet been repaired, I can see. It will soon turn into a family heirloom," said Babu with a laugh so that they would not think he was criticizing them.

He smells so different – almost like a foreigner. Was he always so fair? I can't remember, thought Jamini, as she peeled oranges. She took each segment apart, gently unwrapped the skin and then pushed the seeds out with her thumb. One by one she cleaned out each segment, peering to see if there were any errant seeds in the bowl and then when she had gathered a handful of orange segments, each one stripped of its cover and sparkling with juice, she offered them to Babu. "Ma, I am perfectly capable of peeling an orange," he said, taking a mouthful of orange segments. They did taste damn good like this he thought with irritation. Only Ma had the patience to do this. He could not think of any other woman who would peel fruit in this meticulous way. Certainly not Maria. She would just throw the whole orange at him. "Do it yourself honey." Anyway they did not have this kind of orange in the U.S. ́

"What will you have for lunch, beta?" Jamini asked. She longed to ruffle his hair which now had one or two grey strands but she knew he would not like it. When he was a boy she would oil his hair every Sunday. They would put a chair out in the verandah and as he read a comic book, she rubbed oil into his hair slowly kneading it in so that his head would feel cool. She knew he would never let her put oil in his hair again. He would hate it. There were so many things he did not like anymore – she'd discovered this in the last one week. Though she had cleaned the house till every corner shone, Babu saw dust everywhere. "Can't Kamala see all this dirt? You should get her eyes tested, Ma. Look at those cobwebs. I don't think anyone has cleaned them out for years," he said, his mouth sullen and stained with orange juice. He did not like the new bed they'd had made for the guest room by a carpenter who was Kamala's husband's cousin and who'd done it cheaply. Though the wood was strong now Jamini could see it was not polished well after Babu pointed it out to her. There were so many unpleasant things about the house she had not noticed earlier before Babu came. Now they rushed at her, attacking her as she walked. The curtains she had chosen and stitched herself with so much care, the rug made of waste wool Manish had bought at the craft fair, the ceramic vase her mother had given her for her birthday; everything now looked cheap and tarnished. Babu hated the old sofa which he said looked like something from a dentist's waiting room. But as a child he had loved sleeping on this sofa with his chin tucked into a book. Sometimes, when visitors came, he would pretend to be asleep and Jamini would take them to sit in another room and insist they talk in whispers. The only part of the house he liked was his own room where he shut himself up and worked on his computer which looked like a slim briefcase. "Just let him be. He is busy with his work," Manish said, but once she'd peeped in through the window and saw a row of playing cards gleaming on the screen. A strange tune was playing.

Today she would make coconut sweets with jaggery for him. He used to love them as a child and ate so many once that they had to give him pudin-hara. "Babu, Babu." Jamini whispered with her eyes shut, her hands caressing a plump, sweaty face. She could smell his baby-soft breath, touch his skin that smelt of the Vicks balm she had rubbed on his chest. Every time he fell ill she spent the night sitting by his pillow, gently stroking his head with a damp, scented cloth so that the fever would not rise. She would not leave the room, except to cook his meals till he got well. Manish ate his meals at the office since there would only be plain kitchree at home. "We should all fall ill along with our son and eat only sick room food," he would say but his face would be lined with worry till Babu got well.

"Ma, why don't you talk to Dad about this house?" said Babu

coming into the kitchen, his face dotted with a green paste. "It's going to pieces. Look how badly I've been bitten! I hope these bites don't give me a rash, the guys at U.S. airports are paranoid about Asian diseases. This house is infected with animals, last night I saw a rat or something run past my window!" he said, leaning against the fridge which shuddered with a loud sigh. "Why have you not got rid of this old monster? I told you to. I sent you five hundred dollars last month." Babu touched his face to check if the paste was dry and then looked around for a place to sit. The kitchen was huge, almost as big as his apartment. A row of wooden shelves cluttered with spices, pickles, tin boxes, plastic bottles and half opened packets lined one wall. Trunks were piled up on the other side next to a wicker basket full of lemons. Sacks of onions and potatoes leaned against the trunk and the walls were clutterd with calendars which dated from 1987, 1999 and 2000. "Don't you have a calendar for this year? You do know it is 2002, or has it escaped your notice?" he asked his mother. Jamini smiled and looked up at him. "You naughty boy. Of course I know. Your old mother is not so stupid. It is just that I liked the pictures on the calendars and did not want to throw them away! See I am making jaggery sweets with coconut for you. You like them don't you?" She asked this hesitantly, her hands smeared with warm jaggery. "I don't want anything sweet Ma. I have to watch my sugar. Will you talk to Dad about getting a new place? It would be much easier for you in a modern kitchen with proper fitted cabinets. Look at the amount of junk you have here. I don't believe this. This is my old tiffin box. Ma you are the limit!" Babu picked up the red plastic box which had a faded picture of two children. A boy with brown hair and a girl with golden hair. Behind them stretched a meadow filled with daisies. He didn't know they were daisies till he went to America and saw them in a field. "What are those flowers called?" he asked Maria. "Daisies" she said, surprised at his sudden interest in nature. He wanted to tell her about his red tiffin box but felt shy. Anyway she would not know what a tiffin box was. Here the children ate school lunches much more efficient and hygenic than tiffin boxes with stale, crumpled food. Suddenly Babu remembered the alu parathas Ma would pack in his tiffin box. There was always a different kind of snack for him in that red box. Dad dropped him at the bus stop at six so she must have got up at five to make them. In this shadowy kitchen lit by a single bulb hanging from the ceiling. Sometimes she would even bake a tiny cake for his tiffin and fill it with walnuts and raisins. All the boys in the school tried to grab his tiffin box because most of them brought only sandwiches. "Ma will you make alu parathas one day?" he asked. "But please don't drench them in ghee. I want them to be light otherwise my cholesterol will go haywire like last time," Babu said, putting his arms around Jamini in a clumsy gesture, carelessly tugging at her sari. Jamini's heart leapt with joy. The years fell away as she leaned close to her son. He was in her kitchen demanding food. "I'm hungry Ma… quick. I have to go out to play. Give me something…no, put it in my mouth."

"Today, I'll make parathas for lunch. I will put the alu to boil at once. Taste this. Just one little sweet, you used to help me make them," said Jamini, her voice heavy with sweet, syrupy love which flowed all around her, spilling over the kitchen floor, sticking to the air in fine threads of spun sugar. "No. No, it's too sweet. Listen, please talk to Dad. I have only five weeks left. We can find a buyer or at least start the process. Everything takes so long in India. What with bribes, government permissions etc. It is all so complicated. Once I leave, you guys won't do anything I

know. I mean, it will be too much for Dad," he said, picking up
a sweet absentmindedly. Jamini watched him like a fox watches
a rabbit with hunger and greed in her eyes.

The jaggery sweet, still warm from the fire, melted in his
mouth and stuck to his teeth. When he sat down to work with
his laptop his fingers felt sticky on the keyboard though he had
washed his hands with soap. "Oh shit, I must brush my teeth,"
he muttered and got up. "There must be a thousand calories in
each of those sweets. Ma will make my weight watch programme
go haywire if I give her half a chance." Maria would kill him if he
gained more than a kilo. "I will allow you one kilo of fat because
you are going home and they will want to fatten you like a calf.
But not a gram more. Remember how tough it will be for you
to shed that kilo." They were both on the Atkinson diet and
she would stick to it because she loved meat and did not have
to battle with a Mother who could kill with the most delicious
food. His mind said no each time she offered him something
which was about hundred times a day but somehow his fingers,
his mouth, and his errant taste buds seemed to have a life of their
own and betrayed him each time. The sweet taste of the jaggery
filled his entire mouth though he had eaten one almost an hour
ago and he had to swallow the saliva that surged into his mouth.
"I am drooling like a dog. Must stop this at once!"

Five weeks was a long time. She would make one dish, just
one dish every day at lunch time. He would not realize it but
slowly his body would remember each flavour. "He ate the
jaggery sweet without knowing. Just popped in his mouth like
he used to as a child." Jamini laughed out loud in the empty
kitchen. Yes, one dish from her son's childhood each day would
bring him back to her. Thirty days – that meant sixty meals – it
was enough for her to win his love back. Then maybe he would

come back to live here. They could sell this house but she knew
Manish would never hear of it. He had hated coming to live
here fifty years ago. "I have become a ghar jamai just because
of your whims and fancies," he had grumbled when they moved
in from their tiny flat to look after her father after Ma died. It
was not easy to live in this huge old house with cracked ceilings
and broken floors. The garden was wild with weeds and dark
with tall, ancient trees which did not allow the sunlight to fall
on any part of the house. But slowly Manish had grown to love
this shabby house, made it liveable bit by bit, doing most of the
work himself in his spare time. When Babu was born they spent
all the time the time playing in the rambling garden now full
of the fruit trees Manish had planted. Babu loved the house too
and when his friends came over they would refuse to leave. "Can
we stay, Auntie? This house is the best place to play hide and
seek. There are so many trees to climb," they would say. Now
Babu hated those very corners which he used to hide in so that
none of his friends could find him. But he looked at the world
differently now that he was an adult, an important officer, now
he was called an executive, in a big bank. "My son deals with
billions not just millions of dollars," Jamini had heard Manish
say to his friend one day. But he never praised Babu, never talked
to him anymore. Even at mealtimes, he just sat there reading
a newspaper, his head wrapped in an old shawl. When Babu
asked him a question he would look up blindly as if he did not
understand English. Sometimes she felt ashamed of him but
when Babu looked at him with contempt then she wanted to run
and hide her husband somewhere where her son's gaze would
not scorch him. But now all that would change. She would cook
all the old dishes which Babu would eat, tasting the flavour of
love in each one and their small family would be bound together

in a close circle again. They would laugh and joke as they had done many years ago before Babu had gone away to America. When he was still their beloved son, dressed in clothes she had made for him, with oil in his neatly combed hair and love in his eyes for them. When they could reach out and touch his plump cheeks without fear of offending him, when their old house had been a home and not a germ filled eyesore.

Alu paratha for today, then palak meat, then fish curry with mustard, then eggplant with cottage cheese. Then... Jamini tried to remember other dishes. This would last for just four days.. that was not enough to bring her son back. She had to travel so far to touch him, this was not enough. This would not even be enough to make him remember a slight tinge of the love he had felt for them. He had moved so far, become a stranger she had to pull into the fold again. She had to get past layers of dust from another land which covered his eyes. He could not see them anymore. Futher and further she would have to stretch her arms, look far into the past to pick up the fragments of his love for them which were lying forgotten and mouldy somewhere in his heart. She needed more time, more memories, more food. Babu had loved her cooking so much but a flood of panic hit her and her heart went cold when she could not remember her son as her child anymore.

Three

The women shook their heads and Malarani wiped a tear away. She cried as easily as she laughed. They began to sort the fenugreek leaves, breaking the stems carefully to take some of the bitterness away. Most of the vegetables had been chopped and now sat in a row of bowls. Aubergines, pumpkin, spinach, potatoes, bitter gourd, beans and squash. They could not use any onion or garlic today since it was a funeral feast – it was only at wedding feasts that rich food was allowed. The servants would take the vegetables to the kitchen soon and line them up. For other feasts they were allowed to start the cooking but for this particular one the women had to do everything – chopping, cooking and serving.

But there was still time for another story before they started the cooking. The guests would arrive only at one and there were not that many today. Most people who knew the old man were either dead or too old to travel to Kashipur. It was not easy: first you had to take a train to Kalka, then a tonga or bullock cart to Rajgarh, then a ferry to cross the river. There were taxis too but they charged a lot of money. Hema, who lived with Badibua in the old house, had sat in a taxi only once when her parents had taken her to Haridwar.

Her mother had dreamt again about the old women, now they wanted to go to Haridwar. Hema suddenly started her story before anyone else could. The women were a little surprised by her bold manner but since she was Badibua's maid, they allowed her to speak. Soon they were totally immersed in this strange story. The fenugreek lay forgotten, the tiny green leaves wilting as Hema's story unravelled.

Hema's Story Of Her Mother's Dream About the Dead Aunts

The goat stood still, but its tail was quivering slightly. Somu was not sure whether it was the breeze or the Devta's will. The circle of people who had started gathering at dawn, watched the goat silently and only the Pradhan's wife coughed. Somu turned his head and glared at her but she met his angry look and coughed again, louder this time, gargling the spit in her throat spitefully. Suddenly the goat began to shiver, the drummer boy — who was also the village carpenter — woke up and began to beat his homemade drum in a discordant manner. The goat jumped up with a start, shook its ears and then its entire body began to shake and tremble. It lowered its head, marked with vermilion, and tried to pull the rope which tied it to the pillar but its neck jerked convulsively the other way, entangling it more firmly to the pillar. The crowd began to cheer as the goat kicked up its hind legs, rolled its eyes, showing the white moons and then it gave a loud, hysterical bleat.

Somu let the muscles of his face relax. Standing next to him, his wife let out a faint sigh of relief. The Devta, always benevolent but unpredictable as the rain, had accepted the goat. Now they could take it back and leave it in the temple courtyard with all the other goats which had been offered to the Devta. None could slaughter it and it would grow old with the other sacrificial goats who had shivered under the Devta's all-powerful gaze when the drum began to roll. Those that stood unafraid and still were rejected by the gods and had to be slaughtered and made into prasad. It was only in their temple that this ritual took place: in the neighbouring villages the sacrificial goats were beheaded regardless of whether they stood still or shivered while the Devta decided their fate.

The goat skipped ahead, unaware that it had narrowly missed death. Somu's wife, Parvati prodded it gently with a branch to keep it from running into the mustard fields along the path.

This time the goat had cost him Rs 400. It was all her fault thought Somu, a wave of irritation making his mouth tight now that he was no longer afraid about what the gods would think or do. If she had not dreamt that Choti wanted another goat, they could have used the money to buy some new shoes for their daughter Hema. These days shoes cost such a lot like everything else. It was not easy on a postman's salary to feed four mouths and also keep their various living and dead relatives happy.

It was not as if their own parents, who had died many years ago, made these endless demands. They seemed content wherever they were. The ones they had to please endlessly were Choti and Munni, his late mother's brother's two wives. The two women appeared regularly in his wife's dreams, mostly on full moon nights, to ask for something or the other. Their husband was still alive, now almost a hundred years old but still eating twenty-six puris – fried in pure ghee! – a day. They never asked him for anything or maybe they did but he kept quiet about it. Always a sly man he was.

Last month the women had asked for a pooja and bhog in Haridwar, then before that a feast for the Brahmins and this month they wanted a goat. God knows what they would demand next full moon night...

The village priest said they must do what the spirit asked or else his family would suffer illness or worse, death. "You must make them happy. Dead relatives, especially women, are important. They are not like our parents who have gone to heaven and think only kindly about us. These distant relatives, who were not that kind or generous even when alive, can turn malicious when dead if you do not placate them with gifts," he said taking Rs 51 and a box of sweets for the advice. Somu did not mind giving the women what they wanted, they had had so little while they lived, but he wished they would ask for it all at one time and not make these odd demands which played havoc with his household budget.

His wife sang loudly as they walked and Somu wondered if she was with child again. His youngest daughter was already three years old and maybe this time Devta would give him a son. A son would make his life worthwhile. What was the use of having so much land, a pucca house, five cows and a T.V. if there was no male child to give it to? "Be happy and content, Choti-mami and Munni-mami, make my family healthy and give my wife a son. I will have a feast for you old hags," he said, looking up at the sky. He would not mind spending money on whatever they asked for if they gave him a son. It was not that he did not love his little Hema but a son was a son – a gift from the gods directly to him.

Munni laughed when she heard his words float up through the clouds. "What a sweet boy...always had a smooth tongue like his father. See how he loves me, sent me a goat and now he is planning a feast in my honour," she said, tossing her head back. Her hair which had been white and wispy when she died five years ago, was now glossy black. It hung like a black cloud around her body as it floated in this perpetual silver twilight.

"The goat is not yours, he clearly said Choti mami and we both know that is my name. They are giving it to me to thank me for the good potato crop I sent them last month."

"What rubbish you talk, Choti! You were always stupid and deaf, that is why you never heard the maid servant moaning and singing while our husband made love to her right under your bed in your own bedroom," said Munni jabbing her finger into the space that she knew was Choti.

"There is no need to be rude! Why talk about the past now that we are all dead and our poor husband is still suffering on earth – so feeble and old. All I'm saying is that this goat is mine. See it has my name written on its forehead in vermilion." Munni mami turned her head and gave her husband's wife a dark look which circled around her head and fell like a lasso over it. But all Choti felt was a gentle tug around her neck and she reached up instinctively to adjust the heavy gold necklace she always wore but then she remembered she had no body and smiled.

Munni, irritated by her smug smile, wanted to give her a sharp pinch like she'd done many years ago when they had both been alive. She disliked Choti from the day she had arrived, a fat, dark bride with a hairy upperlip and an enormous dowry. Till Choti had come to their house, she was the main daughter-in-law. Her father-in-law, the randy old goat, had adored her, her mother-in-law listened to her advice and the servants obeyed her. She ruled the household. Her husband, feeble and sick even then, hardly ever spoke to her but it never bothered her till he decided to marry once more because the village faith healer said it would cure him of this mysterious illness. Some said it was epilepsy and others said it was Japanese malaria. Once she had heard the servants whisper that it was the clap he had caught from the village whore. But he could not have gone out of the house, she thought, so she must have visited him sometime. Who knew? But she remembered he was delirious with fever the day Choti, married to him by proxy, landed in their house armed with a clock that chimed, a trunk full of silk saris, five kilos of gold and a big radio which till now only the English sahibs had in Kashipur.

Soon people in the house were swarming around her like flies around a piece of jaggery. Munni was nothing now and even the lowest servant boys talked to her rudely. But then, one day, Choti went out to the rice fields to see a cockfight with their husband who was showing faint signs of recovery, much to everyone's delight. No women were supposed to go to these fights and God's wrath in the form of a bolt of lightning struck the tree she was standing under. She was dead, her neck neatly broken by a branch, before she could call out her husband's name for help and commit another sin. Munni mourned her with the rest of the family, eating salt-less food, sleeping on the ground but her heart sang with joy. Now she could rule the house once more and the chiming clock would be hers forever. But then within a month she too was taken away. A simple operation that old maid doctor had said feeling her insides with a cold gloved hand. It was a simple death instead. In the morning she was alive, giving instructions to the cook, and by afternoon the priest was chanting prayers over her dead body while the servant cooked the funeral rice and lentils from the same rations she had doled out to them.

"What bad luck to lose both daughters-in-law in one month!" everyone said at the joint funeral feast her father-in-law had organized to save money. Their husband, strangely enough, began to regain his health though he took to lying in bed all day. Lazy old goat still alive on earth!

No, she would never let Choti have the goat. It was hers and she would make Somu say so in front of the village. "I send this goat to my beloved Munni mami, my only mama's senior wife." He'd say this loudly and clearly so that even deaf Choti could hear.

Munni thought for a while, letting the fragrant twilight mist circle her body and then pass through her head. "He had asked for a son. I will send him one right now. Sons were so easy to send down. I don't know why they made us hanker and thirst for one all our lives. All you have to do is pluck a male bud from the tree of life and float it down. The winds that travel to the earth every dawn will carry it and Somu's wife can catch it easily in her womb. I will tell her to stand facing in the right direction. In tonight's dream I will give her clear instructions about the goat." Munni tied her hair in a knot in a long practised gesture though her hands did not touch her hair, and then she wafted down to the garden where the tree of life stood. Choti was already there with a male bud in her hand. "Witch! She can read my mind. I must not think of what I'm going to do next," said Munni and shut her eyes, letting her mind go blank. Choti smiled and blew the seed gently towards the winds travelling down to earth. She would send many gifts but better not let Munni know or she would steal her thoughts right now.

She was always so mean to me when we were alive on earth though I never harmed her, in fact, my mother gave her an expensive sari and a gold necklace. "Better keep the senior wife happy or they cast jealous, evil eyes on you," she had said.

I will never give her that goat. Somu will have to give it to me. He owes me a favour. When he was appearing for his B.A.

exams I gave him Rs 500 to buy the question paper from his teacher. Now he struts about, the only B.A. fail in the village. He was very grateful to me when I was alive but now I find he thinks of Munni more. Maybe that stupid wife does not tell him about my messages. What has Munni done for him? She did not have two rupees to give to her maid servants and had to borrow from me. If I had lived long enough maybe she would have asked me to pay for her dentures too! She kept talking about getting new teeth ever since she saw my mother's new set though she had perfectly healthy teeth.

Somu is a sweet boy but too easily swayed by Munni. I must try to get to him. Munni had a year before me to work her charm on everyone in the house though our husband never liked her and preferred to spend every night in my bedroom. Our husband loved only me. That maid was just there when he was heavy with love and I had gone to sleep early. For a sick man he produced a lot of seed. Men must love when they have to or else how will the world go around? Poor man, how lonely he looks now that even the maid has run away from our house!

I wish I had had the time to give him a son, that would have given him some joy. I must remind Parvati that I'm the one who sent her a son. Had to reach so high to pluck him. A nice, plump seed from the topmost branch where the best, healthiest sons grow. Sons who will live beyond their father and light their mother's funeral pyre. Maybe I will send something extra before Munni thinks of it. Gold? Men like gold. How happy our husband was with the heavy gold chain my father gave him! He still wears it though it hangs heavy around his thin neck now. I'm glad he never married again because his new wife would have melted the chain and made some new jewellery for herself. Munni would have done it too but fortunately she is here with me.

Shall I send Somu's wife something? It's not easy to send heavy things like gold since I do not have that much energy. But Munni is new here too and she has the same quota as me. Though she might steal some from the others. She was always so pushy. At my wedding feast she wore a red sari with a heavy gold border and all the jewellery she had. It was not much but it made her look like a bride and confused many guests who gave her the wedding gifts and envelopes with money. My mother was sure she kept some of the money and I have to agree with her now. Why does she want my goat? I must work hard or else she will grab it.

Somu was surprised to see the almond tree full of blossoms. Winter had not left the hills, and the ground was still hard and bare of grass. Yet in his orchard every almond, plum and peach tree was covered with flowers. The bees, confused by this sudden abundance, flew blindly from one tree to another, clashing over the newly opened buds. All the other trees in the village were still bare. Only Somu's orchard glittered on the bleak hillside like a bouquet of flowers and he was pleased and embarrassed by his luck. Then the next day his cows – all five of them – gave birth and a whole new crop of calves arrived. All five were female. Everyone in the village gathered at his house, their faces shining with envy. "It is Choti and Munni mami. I dreamt of them last night, but was not sure what they were saying," whispered Parvati, her eyes bleary with sleep. She went to the corner of the orchard and threw up loudly, scattering the sparrows from the almond tree. "A son this time," thought Somu as he tried to fill every vessel in the house with the milk that was pouring from his five cows. He sent some to the neighbours too.

That season the orchard gave the largest amount of fruit ever, each peach, plum and apricot filled with sweet, fragrant juice, the rice stalks were heavy with seed and the stream below the orchard was suddenly crowded with red, copper and black fish that the village had never seen before. Clouds brought rain just when the wheat crop was about to be sown and then the sun shone brightly to ripen it to pale gold in just a few weeks.

That summer there was no flood or famine in their village, no cows fell down the hillsides, no monkeys attacked the potato crop and no mother stayed awake at night rocking a sick, hungry child in her lap. After nine blissful months Parvati gave birth on full moon night to twins – a boy and a girl. "I must give the Devta a goat," said Somu, cradling his newborn son who had a strange mark on his forhead – like a tiny leaf. "You must give something to Badi and Munni Mami. I feel they are trying to tell me something. Maybe they will be happy with a goat. Get one for each. They never liked sharing, your mother told me, though they were married to the same man."

The two goats stood side by side, their ears touching and did not shiver when the drums began to roll. The Devta did not accept them and when they were slaughtered in the temple courtyard, their heads rolled down the hillside and Somu had to run after them. The meat was tough though it had been cooked with a lot of pure ghee, ginger, fresh chilli paste and sesame seeds. After the Devta was given a small portion the entire village came to eat the prasad except Somu's wife who had to stay at home till her forty days were over. They cooked the meat over a huge fire outside the temple and at dusk the vultures came and cleaned the bones out. But before they could finish, a jackal came and carried the carcass away to the forest. Somu had hidden the goats' heads in the temple storehouse and after smearing red vermilion on their foreheads, he nailed them to the temple doorway as a mark of respect and record of his sacrifice to the Devta. He hoped that Badi and Munnni mami were content now that he had given each one a goat.

Many full moon nights passed, his children grew up healthy and happy but the women never came into his wife's dreams again. The fruit crop was normal and rice and wheat grew well but not with the abundance they had done earlier. The village still talked about that strange summer and wondered what had made it happen. Somu knew but did not say anything but he often asked Parvati if the women had appeared again in her dreams. Somu did not know that they had finally crossed the river of death and flown to a higher circle of twilight where the earth did not exist, and husbands and goats did not matter.

Four

Savitri sorted the rice, carefully picking out the grains of husk. She thought about the time in London when she had to cook bhog for Shivratri once. She kept sorting the rice though there were no husks to be found. They needed a few for the pooja but though they went through a huge pile of rice they could not find a single husk. "You know it is only in our country that the rice has husk," she announced in a loud voice. The women who knew that Savitri had once lived in a foreign country pretended they did not know. They hoped she would tell them about her late husband and his affair with a white woman. But Savitri wanted to tell them how she had cooked the best bhog once. Of course there had been the other two women too, whose names she could not remember anymore.

SAVITRI'S STORY

Though the priest at the temple, Purohit Baba, had asked her to come on an empty stomach, Gita thought the gods would not mind if she had a cup of tea. "I will not put any sugar, only milk. Mahadev liked milk, he will forgive me," she thought as she tip-toed around the kitchen. Gita lived alone now after her husband's death six months ago but she still walked around the house as quiet as a mouse, as she had done earlier when she was always afraid of waking him up. She still thought he was asleep in the upstairs bedroom, his face covered with an old muffler. He would not have liked her going out in the dark alone like this though the temple was only a fifteen minute walk. "A lone woman without a man guarding her is a target for all evil men in this highly civilized country just as she is at home," he would say.

Gita gulped her tea down, trying not to notice its bland sugarless taste. She would make herself a real cup of strong sweet tea when she came back home. It had taken her years to call this tiny doll's house her home though even now she sometimes wondered where she was when she woke up in the morning and heard the police sirens. This tree-shaded, quiet suburb outside London was so different from her huge, noisy, cluttered home in Patna. This entire house would fit into the courtyard at home and there would still be room for poor relatives to sleep and enough space to store the old trunks full of quilts!

Gita walked a little faster, trying not to look at the dark shadows under the trees. Another two streets and she would be at the temple. It would take about four hours to make the bhog though Purohit Baba had said it might take longer. "Do not count the hours when you are serving the Lord of Destruction. He might look at us with his third eye and reduce us to ashes."

Gita shivered with joy when Purohit Baba's voice filled the hall. It was as if God himself had come down to speak to them. The women at the temple said he worked as a cashier in a bank. Every morning after he had done the puja, he changed into a suit that he brought on a hanger with him. Gita had seen him one morning and this new image of the Purohit, in tinted glasses and polished shoes, confused her so much that she forgot to do pranam. He just smiled and got into his car, waving to someone she could not see. The next day he was back as Purohit

Baba, dressed in a silk kurta and dhoti, his noble face lined with sandalwood paste. Gita wiped the other man from her memory and fixed in its place his serene face when he sang hymns to the great Lord of Destruction.

Though the temple was just an empty hall in a school with chairs, dumbbells, and basketballs lined up against the wall, when Purohit Baba sang and his voice rose high, it filled with a divine light, transporting Gita to Shiva's abode in the mountains. She felt so proud when he asked her to help this year with the making of the bhog prasad with wheat flour, almonds and fruit which they would serve after the fasting period was over, though not many people kept the fast here. They were all working, especially the young people and how could you work on an empty stomach? The English people would not understand. She was so surprised when Purohit walked up to her last week. "Ma, you make good shinni I have heard. You may serve the lord this Shivratri," he had said in that wonderful voice of his. As soon as she got home, she had rung up her son in L.A, but in her excitement she forgot to calculate the time difference and he had sounded very irritated. "Mom, it is five o'clock on a Saturday morning! I have had such a rough week, back-to-back meetings. I'll call you later. Take care," he had said before she could give him the news about the Shivratri bhog. The phone crackled in her hand and she tried to bring her son back but he had floated away over miles of ocean.

Just one more street to cross. Gita walked closer to the wall along the pavement, taking care not to go too close to the gates of the houses she passed. English people did not like strangers coming into their garden or even looking into their gates, she had been told by her husband. The streetlamps were still on and a faded grey-gold sun was beginning to rise above the trees. She

could hear sparrows preparing their day and hugged her coat
closer. Her son had sent her this velvet coat last year and though
she did not like its pale blue colour she still wore it when she
went out. It felt good to be able to say, "My son sent me this
fancy coat from America. He is an accountant there in big firm.
So busy all day, god knows what he eats or drinks without me
to take care of him. Just work, work, all day." Gita could see the
school building ahead of her and felt happy. Soon she would be
at the temple. She had once more walked here alone and been
absolutely fine. Each time she managed to do something on her
own she felt she had grown taller and could not stop smiling to
herself. "You are a silly woman," she said and hurried. The shops
were closed and their windows covered with a white curtain. She
knew most of the shopkeepers who called her Mrs Soon instead
of Sen. When her husband was alive she would come regularly to
buy fish and vegetables, take her time selecting the fish but now
she only shopped once a week. She slowed down when she saw
a man curled up under the street lamp, right outside the school
building. She was afraid if she walked too fast he would wake up
and say something to her. But the man continued to sleep, his
head resting on his stomach. "Hope he is not dead, poor creature.
Not a good sign for me to see first thing in the morning,"
thought Gita. No, he could not be dead. In this country no one
died on the streets, not even a stray dog. If some cat or dog was
run over, the police came at once, wrapped the body in a plastic
sheet and took it away. Not like home where the dead bodies
of animals were left for the vultures and kites to clean up. This
man must be drunk. As soon as the shops opened they would
remove him. This was a clean area her husband always said – no
blacks and no peasant Indians from Punjab, just decent, highly
educated families. Her hair was still wet from the bath and she

wished she had not worn this coat. It was quite chilly and what
if she fell ill? Who would take care of her? Her son would not
like it if he had to take leave and come here. Maybe he would
take her to America. There! She had said it. She must not say or
even think of it. He had not mentioned it and her husband had
told her not to ask.

"You must never beg the children for anything."

If she had worn her old black shawl she could have covered
her head with it. Hope the Purohit would not mind that she was
not wearing white. The two other women who were going to
work with her cooking the bhog would certainly wear white since
they were widows. Or maybe they might wear light blue or pale
grey – those colours were allowed. Of course in this country some
widows even wore pink but she would never do that. Her late
husband would be horrified and she did not want to hurt him
wherever he was, may the gods rest him in peace. That is what
they wrote here on tombstones: "Rest in peace."

She did not know the other two women well but had seen
them often during the pooja and various functions at the temple.
At first she had thought Purohit Baba had only asked her to cook
the bhog but then she heard that there were these other two who
would be cooking along with her. She could have managed quite
well on her own and god knows what kind of bhog these two
would cook. She would make the prasad and they could make
the rice. Some women had such a heavy hand when it came to
seasoning. They just threw the salt or chillies in while talking
or thinking of other things. You had to keep your mind quiet,
hold your heart still when you added salt to a dish. That was the
most important part of cooking. You could chop the vegetables
as fine as petals, grind all kinds of spices till they could pass
through muslin but if you added too much or too little salt,

everything was ruined forever. She hoped Purohit Baba would not blame her if anything went wrong. Maybe she should make it clear right from the start. Gita felt a nervous tremble in her stomach. No, why create an unpleasant situation on such a holy day? Mahadev would make everything go right. She said this loudly and walked up the steps. On the pavment the drunk man gave a low groan.

Savitri's hands trembled as she combed her hair. There was not much left to comb she thought, looking at herself in the mirror. At the time of her marriage, her hair hung well below her waist. Her late husband often asked her to wrap it around his neck and then he would bury his face in the dark coils and go to sleep. But that was a long time ago, when she had just arrived in this country – and before he left her for the Mem. They said she had golden hair that was as short as a boy's. "Finally he's got the son he longed for," her brother had joked, but Savitri did not laugh. He was still her husband and she had to respect him. No one could make fun of him in front of her. What if he came back one day and said to her, "Savitri. I have made a mistake. I want to live here with you once more"? Then she would have nothing to feel bad about. She would not feel guilty about making fun of him or saying cruel things about his little adventure abroad. Everyone knew these things happened when men lived abroad. These white women were as beautiful as apsaras who could tempt even the saints. Though this mem was very ugly despite her golden hair. Savitri had seen her photograph in her sister-in-law's house. "This is the one," she said, and then folded the envelope quickly in case she had offended her but Savitri did not feel bad. Later, when she was alone in the room, she looked at the photograph again with a detached curiosity as if it was some stranger who had nothing to do with her or her husband. He had not lived long to enjoy this woman with short hair. God bless his soul wherever he is.

On this auspicious morning she did not wish to think bad thoughts though everyone said he deserved the horrible death he got, falling out of the window like that. They said it was the tenth floor of some hotel in London. She saw his picture in the papers. Nothing seemed to be broken but he was dead. They had spelt his name wrong and said he came from Bangladesh instead of West Bengal. How he would have hated that! The boy-mem was not with him otherwise people would have talked. They still talked in the community saying he was drunk when he slipped and fell out of the window, that he had killed himself but Savitri ignored the wagging tongues. She was soon going home to live with her brother and no one in India would know how he died. Heart attack she would say. No accident or anything. And they would accept that and not accuse her of anything because when a man commits suicide the blame always falls on his wife even if he has left her.

Now that Purohit Baba had asked her to cook bhog, she knew she was safe. He would not have asked if her husband's unnatural death was casting a shadow over her. She would cook such an excellent bhog that people would talk about it for years to come. When she left, they would forget all the cruel things they said about her, her late husband and the poor boy-mem who was now neither a widow nor a wife. These people who gossiped about her would from now on only remember her as the best bhog cook who had worked at the temple. Lord Shiva, who saw everything with his three eyes, would clear her name and then she could go home.

Malti had not slept all night. Her grandson had chicken pox and she kept caressing him with a twig of neem leaves so that he would not scratch himself. "Boys are so naughty," she said to her son before he left for office. Her daughter-in-law luckily had taken a day off today or else she could not have come to cook bhog. She would have died missing out on such an honour. The gods knew how to look after their devotees and her poor beloved Gugu had got chicken pox. She did not wish this illness on him though they said it was better to get chicken pox in one's childhood. Anyway it had given her a free day after a long time. Not that she minded looking after the little jewel. But cooking bhog for Shivratri was a rare gift from the great Lord of Destruction himself. How she missed the pooja days at home where she had been such an important figure. Nothing would happen till she arrived to organize everything. "Malti knows how to do it. We must wait till she comes," Guruji would say to anyone who asked him about the bhog. Single-handed she would cook for a hundred people. She allowed a few young women to do the chopping and cleaning but the main dishes she cooked herself. Measuring out everything carefully with the special silver cup she had and then saying her prayers before adding the last touch of ghee and cinnamon. Pulao for Durga ashtami, khitchree for saptami, paish for navami and then meat for kalipuja. She knew what the goddess liked and when she stirred the huge cauldron the devi's beautiful eyes would watch over her. Everything was different at home. She herself was a different woman: tall, proud and with flashing eyes. Not a soul dared talk back to her, not even her husband who anyway was a kind soul. May Mahadev protect him in his land of death! If he had not caught pneumonia and died suddenly she would still be living at home watching over her ten acres of wheat fields like a queen. Now in this tiny flat she was a clumsy old woman, crashing into everything like an old dim-witted servant who could not remember anything.

Every morning before they left for work her son and daughter-in-law would give her instructions. "Do not fry anything. Keep the front door locked. Do not answer the phone – it is on answer phone. And please Ma do not call the neighbours in for cups of tea. They do not like it. This is not India."

That she knew well. This was not her country. Every minute she wished she were at home amongst her own people. As she walked to the temple – there was no point in wasting money on the bus – Malti played a game she often did. This was the street outside her home in Calcutta. She walked here everyday to go to the fish market. Her maidservant, not the old reliable one but her saucy daughter, followed her with a plastic shopping basket and she had to keep an eye on her so that she would not flirt with the urchin boys who ran behind them shouting, "Coolie, coolie". There was the one-legged coconut hawker shouting in his broken voice, and behind him smoke rose from a cauldron as the shop that sold hot snacks got ready for the day. The blouse shop where you could match any shade of sari, the flower garland maker surrounded by jasmines, mogra, lotus buds and a pile of rose petals, the paan shop, sleepy and quiet at this early hour (later loud music would blare from the radio tucked under the betel leaves) and the sly-eyed ribbons and hairpin man who liked to touch every woman's hands when they paid him, all of them stood by to let her pass. She smiled and nodded at them. "No, nothing today. I am going to the temple to cook bhog for Bholenath. You have tasted my bhog last pooja. It was good was it not? I will get some back for you... don't worry," said Malti with a laugh, holding her shawl tightly around her shoulders so that the crowds jostling down the street, the agitated stray dogs and cows, the beggars still asleep in bundles of rags, would not touch her.

An old lady with a shopping bag which had wheels on it stood outside her house. It was still too early to go out. Her face held a hesitant smile and when Malti passed by she nodded at her. "Nice day. It will be a nice day..." she said, looking at the dark sky. Malti smiled at her and it was only after she had crossed the road that she realized where she was.

They got down to work as if they had known each other all their lives. Each woman knew instinctively what was needed of her and did not ask the other. Gita alone churned the wheat and milk paste as the other two women sorted the rice and lentils out. It was after they had chopped the potatoes and carrots into cubes, sliced the beans into fine strips and shelled the peas, that Gita spoke for the first time. "The potatoes here are so clean with such fine skins but they taste a bit bland," she said, not looking up. Savitri raised her eyes, bright with a look of understanding. "How strange, I was thinking of that too. If only someone would send me a small cauliflower from home. I would eat just one tiny bit every day. My late husband thought it was silly. 'The cauliflowers here are so nice and white', he used to say," said Savitri and thought to herself, like their women. Malti laughed and said, "Yes didi, I would love to have not just vegetables from home but moori and mustard oil, fresh gram, new gur and all kinds of rubbish food we used to eat on the street. My son would kill me if he heard all this. 'You have the best and most hygenic food in this country, how can you long for that filthy, disease-ridden stuff? Hundreds of germs,' he will say. And me, I get up at night and cry sometimes for a bit of chilli and turmeric fried brinjal. Just now I wish I could have one of our rough-skinned potatoes with bits of earth still on it. They taste better, no, the skins fried crisp? Oh, what would Purohit Baba say if he heard us, three old women talking like greedy urchins? Mahadev would not mind I'm sure," she said with a smile.

Gita and Savitri smiled back at her. Then the words began to flow. As they cooked, stirring the huge pots with long-handled 'karchis' which had been brought from home, the three women talked in soft voices. Sometimes they heard each other and then their words disappeared, flowing into the cauldrons to mingle with the simmering bhog. Bit by bit they poured their intense longing for home along with measured cups of hot water, threw in their loneliness with the fragrant basmati rice, sprinkled their forgotten dreams and disappointments carefully along with the salt. A few tears washed the peas, carrots and beans but the potatoes held a tinge of shared laughter. Then they chopped their sadness into fine, almost invisible bits and mixed it with the cinnamon, cardamom and clove powder.

Slowly as the bhog began to bubble, its fragrance rising to fill the entire temple, the empty playground, the silent classrooms, the women fell silent. They dipped a ladle in to taste the bhog. It needed a little something sweet. With a gentle twist of their fingers all the three women placed their palms on top of each other, like fish making love and poured in all the love that remained in their hearts. They wrung it out, squeezing, till it flowed like a stream into the cauldron, spilling on the floor, staining the clean white tiles. When the bhog was served the people who gathered for the feast at the temple were surprised at the rich flavour and Purohit Baba smiled quietly and said, "It is only the Lord's benevolence."

Five

The hibiscus shrub had finished flowering but one lone flower still clung stubbornly to the lowest branch. Just below the shrub, in a shallow hastily scratched dusty bowl, sat a dull brown hen, her wings tucked neatly under her stomach. The crimson red flower dangling right above her ruffled head gave her a false and somewhat lopsided bird of paradise appearance. She was fast asleep and the rooster's incessant calls made no difference to her. The crisp winter sunlight made the shabby backyard with its dusty plants look much brighter this morning and even the discarded old furniture had taken on a gleaming patina quite pleasing to the eye. The rooster gave one more lament and flew up clumsily to sit on the wooden fence that divided his patch from the neighbour's garden. From there he watched his enemy.

Jogen stood on the roof of his two-storied, freshly painted house and glared at the rooster with puffy eyes. "Let the bastard even think about flying into the garden and I will wring his neck," he muttered to himself, taking a sip of lukewarm tea to soothe his throat before he gave his first warning cry of the day. How beautiful his roses looked this morning he thought, keeping a wary eye on the rooster.

His garden, though only a small one, was an oasis in this desolate street where every other backyard was a patch of moth-eaten rugs, dying plants, old furniture and discarded tyres. Jogen was the village postman, a proud third generation government employee. He still had his grandfather's cap with its gold embroidered emblem of the Royal Mail. He loved the soft faded woollen cap and often wore it secretly at night, savouring the delicious pangs of guilt. "I am not being unpatriotic, just faithful to my grandfather's memory, the first postman of Dhompur," he chanted, stroking the emblem with his fingertips, tracing the intricate pattern. Of course he would never betray his country and government by wearing this English cap in public, no, not even in front of his wife.

There were many things Jogen did not do in front of his wife, a plump, sharp-eyed girl who everyone said was young enough to be his daughter. Some whispered it behind his back while others, like his mother, had said it to his face. He took no offence at this since it was the truth. Soni was the same age as his daughter from his late wife and he clearly remembered the day both the girls were born. Soni's father was a good friend of his, a kind and generous man who died in his prime, choking over a betel nut at his son's wedding. Some guests, his side of the family mainly, said he was poisoned by Soni's mother but why speak evil of the dead even when some late people deserved it. Soni, unfortunately, took after her mother, who was a loud woman with a big mouth which was always open like a tiny red cave to let out a stream of words, raucous laughter or take in endless amount of food. Yes, he could see Soni growing more like her mother each day.

The white rose bush was doing really well, each branch laden with heavy bunches of roses falling in a curve which almost touched the ground. Though there was no scent in the flowers, the bees loved to hover around the rose bush. He would try and plant another one of the same variety but with pink flowers. Maybe he would go to the Koti nursery and get one next time he had to go to the head office. At the end of the month when it was pay day. Yes, he could go on pay day and get some manure too. There was a new English kind made with crushed bones. Bone-meal it was called. But was it all right for vegetarians to use this manure made with dead animals? Jogen pondered over this with a deep frown. He was not eating it, was he? Only giving it to the roses so that they could grow healthy and produce more flowers. It was like feeding special food to a pregnant woman. No harm done. But if his mother was alive he could never have brought the bone manure home! Not even talked about it. What a scene she had created when Dhani opened his butcher's shop though it was far down the road, screaming abuses at his wife, cursing them so that they could never have a son. Her curses seem to have worked and poor Dhani managed to produce only a daughter. So what if he was a butcher, he had to earn a living like everyone else. Not everyone could get a good government job in the post and telegraph service like him. He was a lucky man – if only the rooster would leave his roses alone and Soni would give him a child. The rooster seemed a bit off colour today and was not strutting about like he did every morning. He just kept calling out in his harsh voice as if he was complaining about something. As long as he kept to his side of the garden it was all right.

Jogen rubbed his chest and thought, even a daughter would be better than no child. A lovely little girl who would gather the roses and talk to him. There was a flutter under the rose bush and Jogen leaned forward to see what it was. The stray cat who lived in the ditch outside their garden, had arrived to inspect the rubbish heap now. That would keep the rooster away for a while. Why was he not happy to stay in their patch, with their rubbish and that single hibiscus plant which caused a ripple of envy in Jogen's heart each time it burst shamelessly into flower. No one looked after it, watered it, dug the earth under it or even admired it from that house yet it was always producing bright crimson blossoms. Maybe it liked all the rotting flesh and blood on the ground that the butcher brought to throw here.

He wished Dhani would not throw the bloodied chicken heads, claws and innards into his patch. Bad enough to have those wretched chickens roaming around the house, clucking all day long. Dead they were even worse. Sometimes he could smell the fresh blood from Dhani's patch floating right up to the roof.

"Haaaah..harraaaeeee...mmmeee," he shouted as the rooster rose from the fence and flew down to his rose patch. A bit of tea spilt down his chin and he quickly wiped it as his wife came up the stairs. He could hear her panting heavily, her numerous bangles making a tinkling sound but he did not turn around. The rooster was still in his rose patch, strutting about and leaving a trail of droppings behind him. "Let the poor creature be! Anyway, they say chicken shit is good for plants," Soni said and came up to stand close to him. He could smell her strange feral smell which was strongest at this time of the morning. Soni broke a green twig off the jasmine he had planted in a flower pot and began picking her teeth. As the flowers fell one by one from the broken twig, she raised her head and twisted open her mouth. Jogen did not look at her but he knew she was rolling her tongue around her mouth, jabbing it deep into her cheek and then she would spit loudly in the flower pot. He saw the leaves tremble and said, "I have told you not to do that so many times. Now you will say that your spit is good for my jasmine plants." This in the patient voice which he used to talk to his wife. Soni stretched and raised her arms above her head as she yawned. Her kurta was torn under the armpit and he could see a soft curly patch of hair peering out.

"Haaa ttt aa ja ja..." he shouted once more and this time picked up a small piece of wood from a pile he kept under the flower pots only for this purpose. Wooden chips were a good missile since they would not kill the bird but frighten it away, at least most of the time. He aimed it at the rooster but it missed and fell on his rose bush instead, scattering a cloud of white petals. Soni clucked her tongue in irritation and clapped her hands, her bangles jangling loudly. The rooster, startled, began to run and then flew up suddenly and crossed over to his side of the patch.

"I am going to oil my hair, wash it and then cook lunch. It will take time. So have something to eat now," she said and went down the stairs. As the sound and smell of his wife receded Jogen gave a sigh and began watching his roses again. Later he would go down and pick up the broken one.

Soni picked up the bowl of oil she had kept in the sun to warm and began slapping it on her head. Then she parted her hair carefully and rubbed a bit of warm oil in each section, humming under her breath. "Lotus-eyed beloved...come to me beloved mine..." she sang in a tuneless voice, watching the fence which separated her husband's garden from her lover's patch. Dhani must be still asleep, the lazy swine she thought, a ripple of warmth tingling her skin as she thought of Dhani's large body sprawled on his bed. She blurred his wife' s face which suddenly appeared next to him on the bed. Bloody woman, why does she not go back to her mother's house? She is going to drop that baby any day now...the scrawny bitch. She had not met Dhani for four weeks and five days now. They saw each other everyday across the fence or outside on the street, or near his shop. But what use was that? They had to be together, skin to skin, breath to breath otherwise it was as good as not seeing him. He could be a stranger for all she cared. "Go home, you bitch...go and breed another ugly black female child – Mother...my goddess make it another girl. Please...do not give her a son...please Devi. I will fast every Friday for you – do not give her a son..." Soni shook her hair and picked up the bowl of oil, now quite warmed by the sun, and poured the remaining oil on the top of her head. She shut her eyes and gently rubbed her scalp with her fingertips, the oil making a soothing chapp...chapp sound on her scalp. Then she wiped the bowl with the ends of her hair and turned her back to the sun to let the oil soak in. Soon she was fast alseep.

She dreamt not of her lover – the handsome, eagle-eyed butcher Dhani – but of his thief rooster and her husbands's white roses. They were sitting in Dhani's bedroom, she and another woman, maybe his wife. A table covered with food was before them. In the middle next to a bouquet of white roses lay the rooster – now simmering in a rich, almond studded curry. Soni could not bear to eat the curry yet the other woman, she was sure it was Dhani's wife as a young girl, was eating it greedily, tearing the flesh with her hands.

The sound of the cock crowing woke her and for a second she panicked, then when she realized she was in her own courtyard and not in her dream or in Dhani's bed with the first light of dawn streaming in through the window, she cursed under her breath. The oil, cold and clammy now, was trickling down her forehead and she wiped it off with the end of her duppatta. She put a cauldron of water on the fire, wrapped an old shawl around her shoulders and then sat down to watch the steam rise with half-closed eyes. Before his wife came, she used to meet Dhani every night. She would wait for Jogen to fall asleep, counting hundred till his breath became even and low. Then she would climb to the terrace in her bare feet, licking her lips to make them moist and red, she would raise her salwar and jump over the low wall. Sometimes Dhani would be waiting for her at the window, his body eager and urgent but there were many nights when he would be snoring gently, his arms folded neatly over his stomach, the moonlight making him look like the corpse of a saint. She would wake him gently and be rewarded with a sleepy embrace.

Then the night would pass too soon and the wretched rooster would begin to crow. She would rush back to the terrace, vault over the wall and crawl into her bed, pulling the covers over her head. Jogen would always be asleep, his face turned to the wall.

But those nights seemed so long ago. One whole year ago. Now his wife was there in his bed, breathing heavily, moaning as the child stirred in her womb. His young daughter, hardly one year old also slept in the same room and Soni would often see her crawling about on the terrace. If she and Jogen had a child he would never treat her like that! Five years had passed but they had no child, despite Jogen's clumsy fumblings in the dark and her ardent prayers to the goddess of the womb, many offerings to the goddess of barren women, to the tree shrine, to the dumb Babaji.

Now, maybe, Dhani would give her a child. Surely the love she felt surge through her veins would bring fresh blood into her womb. Sometimes, when no one was around, they would steal a kiss in the corner of the garden where they threw the rubbish. There amongst the dead chickens bones, and feathers, rotting flowers and dry cowdung cakes, he would quickly squeeze her and pinch her lips till she cried out in pain.

Dhani was not a real butcher. He explained to her when she met him for the first time on the terrace on his daughter's naming ceremony. "I buy the chicken and goats from the mandi, selecting only the best. I never touch them, just point with my stick. My boys clean and cut them and get them ready for the shop They are low caste and very poor so it does not bother them if their hands get bloody," he said, laughing in that shrill way he had. Yet whenever she looked at his plump, slightly crooked hands, caressing her, squeezing her flesh, she would see them wringing a chicken's neck.

Soni heard her husband coming down the stairs and threw some rice into the boiling water. She would wash her hair later, what did it matter if it looked all oily and unclean. Jogen never even looked at her except when he was startled by something rude she said. These days she did not care enough to annoy him."O Dhani.. send her away..." she whispered over the hissing cauldron.

"The rice is not cooked properly," said Jogen, looking down at his plate.

"Then cook it yourself, I have no time to put up with your fussing – drink the lassi and don't whine," said Soni but her heart was not in her curt words. Any other time she would have loved to get into a quarrel with her husband so early in the day because that meant she could sulk all day till late at night and go to sleep in the other room. This gave her a chance to get away to the terrace earlier; but of what use now to sulk when the bitch was still stuck like a leech next door?

I will make some halwa and send it to her. That will make her have false labour pains. I will smother the semolina with pure ghee, almonds, dates, and raisins. Maybe add some chilli powder – with lots of sugar – she won't know. It will make the wind rise in her belly and she will think it is her time and run farting to her mother! Hai...that is what I will do, she thought, her eyes blazing with malice. Suddenly the cock crowed outside though it was noon and Soni laughed out loud as her husband spilt his glass of lassi on his lap.

"You should have not taken the trouble sister," said Dhani's wife breathing heavily as she put her hand out for the plate of golden halwa. "No, no, one should feed a pregnant woman – the gods will bless one," said Soni, narrowing her eyes. "Eat it while it is hot – I will make some more tomorrow," and by the day after you will head home my sweet sister Soni thought, as she jumped over the wall. She could have gone downstairs and come up but she loved vaulting over the fence just to keep in practice. Placing one bangled wrist on the ledge she would twist her body and leap gracefully over the brick wall in one quick movement. What a pity Dhani could not see her athletic prowess but his stupid wife watched her with her mouth open, a handful of halwa gleaming in her fist.

For one week she sent halwa every morning to her rival but nothing happened. The woman had a cast iron stomach and digested even the raw leaves of senna she had put in to give her wind. Then, just when Soni was giving up hope, the halwa worked its magic and on the ninth day, at the first light of dawn, just when the cock began to crow, Soni heard the first scream through the thin wall which separated their houses. "Ma... Mai...help, the pains have come...ma..." began the wail. Soni leapt out of bed. "What...what..." mumbled Jogen. "I must go next door, she needs help," she said, pulling her duppata over her head.

Dhani was snoring in his usual saintly position while his wife crouched at the foot of bed, groaning. She did not dare touch him to wake him up or call out his name since it was forbidden. She was his wife but since Soni was not she was not bound by any rules so she shook him rudely and said "Arree wake up...take you wife to her mother...I think her time has come..." Dhani stared at her stupidly and then jumped out of bed, clumsily tripping over a fallen pillow. "My God you...you...how did... you..." he stuttered looking for his wife who was now lying on the ground. Together they picked her up and put her on the bed. "Stay with her, I will get a rickshaw..." said Dhani and stumbled out blindly. "Ma, ma..." moaned Dhani's wife clutching Soni's hand and pressing it to her stomach. "Don't leave me...please don't go..." Soni felt her heartbeat thumping wildly against her palm. What was her name? She had never asked Dhani his wife's name. "There ... there, sister...stay calm...do not fear... we will take you to your mother soon...hush." She had stopped moaning now and her eyes were half shut. In another hour she would leave the house to go to the hospital or her mother's – who cared – and tonight she would come to this room and take her rightful place in this bed. Oh, the joy of being with him again. Suddenly, without warning, the baby moved under her hand and Soni moved back in fear. Dhani's wife seemed to be half asleep now, tears staining her face. Had she fainted? Soni tried to shake her and then suddenly she gave a loud cry and sat up as her clothes were drenched in water. Then she began to cry, her hands over her ears, trying to shut out Dhani's wife's screams of pain. "Oh Devi... don't let her die. I did not ask you for this... please let her live...." She tried to hold Dhani's wife but she thrashed about pulling her down like a drowning person. Where had that idiot Dhani gone? The streets were crawling with rickshaws. Where was he? Then suddenly with a piercing cry Dhani's wife arched her back, lifted her stomach in the air and came down with a crash. She bit her hand. There was blood on the sheets and the little girl hiding behind the door began to sob and then she heard another cry — a baby's wail. Soni could not bear to look down but forced herself. It was something she had seen thrown outside Dhani's butcher's shop — a bundle of flesh, blood and mucus. She recoiled but something forced her to touch it — but it was attached by a bloody rope to Dhani's wife. Soni felt the room spin and then her head filled with the baby's wailing cries, she hit the ground.

The rose bush had lost all its flowers in the storm that blew through the village at night. A freak unseasonal storm but a good omen since it brought the rains early, said every one. And Dhani's new daughter, now nine months old, was thanked for this bounty. His wife had wanted to call her Soni since it was Soni, kind generous Soni, who had brought her into this world. Fed her magic halwa and delivered the child all alone. But for some reason Dhani did not agree and called her Seema instead.

Soni sat in her garden near the rose bush and cleaned a plate of rice. Her hair gleamed in the shadow of the rose bush like polished ebony and the rooster eyed her from his perch on the fence. Jogen watched her from the terrace guarding her from the rooster. Dhani watched her too from his patch but she now looked at him as if he was a stranger. Anyway, a woman big with child had no charm for him.

Six

Shashi suddenly started laughing and all the other women — they had no idea what had made her laugh — looked at her and smiled. "Masi, when you were telling us that story about those women in London, I suddenly thought of my friend Sona. That girl was completely mad! Her poor husband tried so hard to teach her English so that she could be a bit modern and go to parties with him. But she hated learning it and when she found out he was cheating on her… you'll never believe what she did," said Shashi and she looked at them, a naughty glint in her eye. She knew the women would be shocked when she told them about Sona, but there was no harm. Let them know a little bit about the world outside their kitchen. It will give them a thrill. And anyway she was tired of chopping vegetables now.

Shashi put the knife down and began her story.

SONA'S STORY

The dust laden winds carried a scent of rain when Sona rose at dawn to check her husband's trouser pockets. She dug her hand deep into the pockets, feeling the soft lining with her fingertips. Both were empty but later when she turned them inside out and shook them out before throwing them into a plastic bucket full of soapy water, a crumpled ball of paper fell out. She opened it out carefully, smoothing the edges with her wet, slippery hands…it looked like a cinema ticket. "Love and God" the ticket said. Sona read slowly holding the pink piece of paper against the window as if the sunlight would make it easier for her to read the washed out letters.

Her English was still not very good though she had been trying to learn how to read and write for two years now. As soon as she learnt a new word, saying it over and over in her head all day long, the ones she had learnt earlier escaped from her mind. She could only carry one word of English at a time, storing it in her head where it sat like a ball of lead, giving her a constant dull headache.

Gautam had given up trying to teach her. "Your head is like a block of wood. Not a word I say goes into it," he had shouted, throwing the Rapid English Reader-Part 1 out of the window. Sona had brought it back into the house, dusted the earth off its covers and wiped the picture of a pretty boy and girl on a swing. Then she stored it in her saree cupboard under the starched cottons so that it would remain flat. She took it out sometimes in the afternoons when the house was quiet and amah, her maid was asleep in her quarters, and looked at the pictures. The boy and girl she loved but their parents she thought were a little cold and snobbish. The father always wore a false smile and the mother looked like one of those women who would never share a recipe with you or might give you the ingredients but leave one important thing out. The letters, written in bold on the first page of the book, were familiar now to her and though she did not know what they meant when they were written together, she could recognize each one separately. M she liked best because it reminded her of a small bridge, S too was one of her favourites since it could be written easily and she saw it was used in many words, usually at the end. X frightened her and Z she thought had something evil about it. When she looked at the letter, turning the book around, it looked liked a serpent about to strike. A, b...c...d...f...z... o...b... English, English, English, she sang when she bathed but she never spoke to Gautam about these funny letters that whirled about in her head because he was hardly ever at home.

She could have spoken to him in those early days of their marriage when he used to try to speak to her in English, especially when they made love. "Darling, darling...sweetheart..." he would whisper and later, when he lay with his head on her breast, smelling of her, he would explain to her what they meant in Hindi. But she had not paid much attention to the strange words then because her mind had wandered far away from her body. Anyway her head was always so heavy with a delicious languor in those far away times. "I will teach you English, my sexy little peasant, you wait and see how quickly you will learn," he said to her, laughing. They used to laugh a lot those days.

The she-cat was around even then though Sona had recognized her scent only a few months ago. Hers was the main scent though sometimes there were others too, but her musky odour rose above the other faint scents demanding immediate attention and that is why Sona had named her she-cat.

She had not been afraid of her then.

There had been talk at home about some girlfriend. "There was a girl, some Anglo-Indian but then Gautam's mother threatened suicide and all that love-shove nonsense was buried," her sister told her a few days before her wedding. They had laughed then because everyone had a lost love tucked away but marriage was something your parents decided for you. The old love faded away like a dried flower pressed in a book. Years later you opened the book and tried to remember the scent. But Gautam had not done that. His love had not been buried at all. He had brought it with him to their married life and Sona saw it everyday on her husband's sullen face, smelt it on his body, read it in his indifferent eyes. All he had done was keep it aside for a few months while he explored her and then like an old disease that lay dormant in his body, it had resurfaced, maybe stronger than before.

Sona had seen the she-cat once in a shop. A thin boyish face with short hair. She hardly had any breasts Sona noticed quickly before she turned but there was something very unusual about the slow yet sudden way she moved. Like an animal waking up after a long sleep, relaxed yet totally alert to any danger. Gautam had said something to her in English and she had walked away with a laughing look at Sona. Though she had not come close to them, Sona could smell her special scent as her eyes followed her till she disappeared. Gautam was very nice to her that day, bought her a new saree and sat patiently while she chose a matching blouse. At first she had thought the she-cat was the only one around but gradually she could smell the other women too.

Sona roamed the house at night, repeating the alphabet and wondering if it was safer for her husband to sleep with one woman or a crowd of women. Each woman had a different scent. One smelt of stale roses, another seemed to have bathed in mustard oil. One day she smelt a new one that had drenched herself in sandalwood along with some foreign perfume. She attacked Gautam that night, crying and whimpering and forced him to make love to her. Sona suddenly started laughing. All the women were standing around the bed, watching, waiting for Gautam to finish. She heard them whisper and giggle right next to the bed, filling the room with their clashing scents. Sona did not mind the she-cat, after all she had been there right from the beginning but she hated and feared the others because she could not see their faces. "One extra woman – outside the marriage, there is no harm," she heard her mother say. "You know he is a rich man. In the olden days all important men had to have a mistress whether they wanted to or not. No one respected them if they stayed at home with their wives. Why, your grandfather had two mistresses. My mother invited them to my wedding, of course they never came but sent a gift. I forget what it was – something heavy, pure gold. You should not mind. He gives you enough money to run the house plus whatever extra you want for jewellery and sarees. Let him have her, takes the pressure off you, you know…his demands in bed, but he should not have more than one woman. That may complicate things and god knows which of them might get pregnant. One you can keep track of, but two or more mean trouble for sure. You should try quickly for a son. That will tie him down to you forever. Nothing like a male child to rope in a roving husband," she said. "Buy and buy. Shopping really helps you to feel better." So Sona began to buy.

She had hundreds of sarees with shawls and bags to match, two refrigerators with automatic defrost, a microwave, five T.V sets, three cars and two drivers. They had a cook but Sona liked to cook all the meals. "The only thing he likes about me now is my cooking, so I will not give that up," she told her mother when she scolded the cook for watching T.V while Sona made puris in the kitchen. The she-cat could not cook. Sona was sure because she was educated and everyone knew that educated girls could not cook. Sona had been to school but her grandmother ordered her father to take her out when she turned ten. "I do not want her to wear short skirts and show her knees to the whole world. She has learnt enough. She can read and write Hindi, count in English till hundred. What more is needed for a woman? The more you let them study the more difficult it will be to find a good boy for them. Already she is so tall and her skin is not very fair either. Education will weigh her down even more heavily." So Sona left school and began to learn how to cook a rich curry without using onions or tomatoes, make pickles out of every known vegetable, embroider endless tablecloths which were never used since they ate on the kitchen floor.

Gautam's father and her father were childhood friends. Their marriage was arranged when Gautam was five and she yet to be born. "If my next child is a daughter, she belongs to you," her father had said though he was scolded later by his mother, her grandmother. "You fool, do not be in such a hurry to ask for a female child. You have only two sons so far." Sona was actually promised to Gautam's older brother, but he ran away to Bombay to join films. Some said in the village that he had married a Muslim girl. Gautam's family spoke about him in the past tense, reading his letters aloud as if he had written them posthumously, their voices sad but respectful.

Gautam was married while he was still in college "before he grows wings" his father said when they brought the engagement sweets and sarees. Sona did not really see much of him in her first year of marriage because he went away to England to study further. Maybe that is where he got a taste for white girls with short hair. Like a tiger who has tasted human flesh and cannot do without it, Gautam too was addicted to alien flesh. Her body was too much like his own, they belonged to the same religion, caste, village and even looked alike. She bored him like his mother and sisters did with their familiar faces and dull everyday talk.

Sona picked up the cinema ticket which had dried crisp in the sunlight. She held the stiff blurred-with-black-dots ticket in her hand and saw Gautam in the cinema hall, his handsome face half lit in the dark, his mouth open as he watched a kissing couple in an English film. The she-cat's head rested on his shoulders, her short hair gleaming like a silken cap. Sona went to the cinema once in a while with Gautam's mother and they always saw a religious film. During the interval when the lights came on, Sona's mother-in-law would take her prayer beads out and chant loudly. Once she carried a huge bag of sweet puffed rice and Sona had to pass it down to the entire row. Then the usher came and stopped her but he too took some in his cupped palm. When the film was over and they were leaving the hall people came up, did a namaste to her and some touched her mother-in-law's feet. It was a happy day for both of them.

Sona folded the cinema ticket before putting it in the drawer where she kept all the other evidence of Gautam's love affairs. Three green beads (glass), a hair clip (for short hair), a lipstick stained handkerchief, a bracelet (artificial not gold), and several bits of paper with names written in English. These Sona was not sure about but since they had a strong scent, she stored them with the other items. As she placed the cinema ticket, Sona saw that the drawer was quite full. When she had started collecting these items of her husband's unfaithfulness Sona did not know what she would do with them but it made her feel good to keep them safely. This way she could control the situation. Locked up in the drawer these tokens of her husband's desire for other women, could not spread their scent and maybe they would shrivel up and die. Then she would bury them one by one in the garden. She could burn them too but then the smoke would carry their scent all over the house and then he would inhale it too and it might bring the longing back into his heart. No, it was best to keep them locked in this small drawer.

Then one day, to ward off the evil eye which sometimes stared at her when she touched the other women's things, she began offering the tokens to the gods. "I must give money with them or else the gods will not accept these silly, cheap things. And I must steal the money from him. It will be like a fine. Then the gods will not punish him for being unfaithful to his wife."

At first she took only the small change lying on the table where he kept his car keys but as days went by, the gods wanted more. Today she had taken Rs 50 from his shirt pocket. This week's total was quite a lot. That five hundred rupee note in the old jacket he had asked her to send to the drycleaners was a windfall. That would settle the score for the cinema ticket. The gods were not unfair and they only wanted a fair exchange. Each piece of evidence had to be compensated with money or the gods would get angry and strike them dead. Or worse take her unborn baby away. The baby understood English when she spoke to it and kicked her playfully.

Till now she had managed to settle the score, keep the balance, but it was getting difficult. Gautam never noticed the missing money but now the gods wanted to be paid in cash and on the same day she found any evidence of his cheating. Today's cinema ticket was paid for and the gods appeased but who knows what she would have to give them tomorrow.

Sona closed the drawer and walked out into the garden. It was still hot though the sun had set. Gautam would be home late again. His secretary, she was also one of them Sona was sure, had rung to say he had a late meeting. "Sir said please do not wait for dinner, he will eat something in the canteen," said the girl.

Sona wondered if this conversation could also be taken as evidence and she would have to pay a fine for these words too.... No that would not do. The gods only wanted something that she could hold in her hands. Not thoughts, not voices and not scents, thank god or else she would go mad trying to pay all the fines.... The house was full of scents all day, swirling around her head and filling her nose, her mouth and ears. She must run around all day and try to pay for the scents. "Run...run," she shouted. She had read it in the English book. "Run...run... run."

Seven

Late Banurai Jog looked at the women and smiled. He had just learnt to smile recently and tried to practise it as often as he could. It was much easier now that he was dead and this new place he was in was so full of wonderful things. Actually if you looked closely there was nothing here to smile about, yet he felt happy and at peace just like the women below. How comfortable they looked sitting around in a circle surrounded by vegetables, chatting merrily to each other. He hoped he would be born a woman the next time around. He was probably the first man to wish that. They said only sinners were born as women – and sometimes as dogs. He was happy to be born as either. He was not sure how long it would be, but he was prepared to wait here, happily suspended in time. Sometimes he could look down and see things happening, and listen to voices but most of the time he remained suspended in ether.

Jog peered through the clouds. The women seemed to be preparing for some kind of a feast. Maybe it was for him. Was it that time already? It seemed like just the other day that he was sitting in the very courtyard the women were preparing for his death anniversary feast. He had made the right decision, leaving the house and the farm to Mala's cousin Badi instead of his son who would have sold it at once. And then, maybe he'd have bought a bigger post office in England. Jog smiled. He did not hate his son anymore but neither did he feel any love for him. He just let him be who he was.

Jog looked past the women towards the garden. The flowers he had planted were in full bloom now and the guava tree was laden with fruit. As he floated above it, inhaling its sweet fragrance, he thought about the time he had walked there, the earth wet and cool under his feet.

LATE BHANURAI JOG'S STORY

Jog hated the flowers. His son, who could not come for the funeral, had sent a huge bouquet of evil looking white flowers from London. Jog was not sure whether the flowers came all the way from London or were sent by a florist in Delhi. Mala would have known such things but she was not here. And he would never know now.

He did not really care where the flowers came from and wished they had not sent them – Raman and his shopkeeper wife. He hated them, their white, cruel petals which were shaped like claws filled him with revulsion. Their heady, sweet fragrance, artificial like the expensive perfumes many fast women used, filled every room in the house and made him nauseous. A swarm of tiny midges had settled deep inside the flowers, scarring the fleshy white petals with black spots.

He had told the servants to throw the bouquet and its unopened letter into the garbage heap at the far end of the garden but they had kept it somewhere because the breeze carried the scent, now stale and sweeter, into the house for days, till he asked the mali to burn them in the rubbish bin. But when he came into this room where Mala had died, he could still smell the flowers, burnt and rotten. Someone must have hidden one flower under her pillow.

Mala had been a good wife to him, quiet, well-behaved and obedient. She had looked after him for thirty years, putting up with his dark moods and keeping the world at a safe distance. Their son had gone away to live in England: though trained to be an engineer with offers of jobs from many prestigious firms, he worked in a post office shop. His wife's father, an uneducated immigrant from Punjab, owned it and when he died Raman had decided to take it over. Jog could not believe it when the letter arrived to tell them that Raman had quit his job and was going to sell stamps, butter and sugar. His only son, a qualified engineer from IIT, Raibahadur Verma's only grandson, was now a full-fledged shopkeeper in some terrible working class area outside London. Fortunately all this happened when both his parents had passed away, otherwise he would never have been able to tell them this shameful thing. The other relatives made snide remarks but no one had the guts to say anything to his face. They probably did to Mala but she never said anything about it.

Three years ago Jog had gone to England to help an old client – the Raja of Jaunapur – with a tax case the Indian Government had slapped on him. Mala had just found out about the lump under her armpit and did not want to travel. She had never wanted to go anywhere except to Delhi to visit her family but he made sure that was just once a year for ten days. The driver dropped her and then he went back exactly after ten days to fetch her. Her mother never asked her to stay longer and neither did any members of the family inquire about him. They were polite and friendly if he happened to answer the phone when they rang for Mala, only on Sundays, but they understood that he liked to keep his distance. He could sense from their hushed voices that they respected him greatly. It made him feel good. But he kept his guard up in case they got more friendly.

Mala had asked him to meet Raman and his wife. She had just started her course of chemotherapy and her voice trembled as she spoke. "Please give them these – a few old pieces of jewellery and a silver framed photograph of Raman as a baby. They might like to show them to his children when they have them." She looked away as she spoke. "I will not be around to see them but what does that matter. They don't need my care. They will grow on their own like my plants," she said and then began to pack his suitcase, folding each shirt in a thin muslin bag so that it would not get creased. She did it slowly, her thin fingers moving over the cloth like some graceful winged creature. Jog shut his eyes to bring her shadowy face closer to him. But there was nothing but a square of light from the window imprinted in his closed eyes. He got up and walked out of the house into the garden. He felt someone was watching him but when he turned around there was no one.

It was just the driver who stood up, startled by his sudden appearance. Jog waved him away and then went back to the house. The day seemed to stretch ahead endlessly as he walked around the empty rooms. What had Mala done all day? When their son was a baby there was probably something to do though the amma was there to do everything. Then he was sent to boarding school, the same one Jog had been sent to at the age of six. What did she do then all day? Sleep, read, eat, walk. He was at work all day and never asked her. Jog tapped his foot on the wooden floor, tracing its lines.

How had she filled all these hours that now weighed him

down? Did she have a secret that made time fly and months go past without you noticing ?

Jog walked into Mala's room, slowly moved the curtains aside in case the flowers were hidden there. Their invisible scent was irritating him

He had felt so ashamed and angry to see his son standing behind a counter, handing out packets of tea and sugar to old English ladies, joking and laughing as if he had known them all his life. Some argued with him about the price, calling him an Indian dacoit. "Thugee, that's what you are," and he teased them about being misers. "What are you hoarding all that money for, my love? Planning to run away, are you?" His wife, a sullen girl with a slight squint in her eyes, sat behind a little caged cubicle selling stamps and weighing envelopes, holding them against the light to check what was in them. "I made you an engineer, sent you to England, yet you prefer to be a shopkeeper," he said trying to keep his voice low. Raman had laughed and winked at a young English girl who had come into the shop. "Come in love, meet my Dad from India. He is giving me his favourite lecture." The girl had smiled at him and put her hand out. But Jog had walked out of the shop, blinded by a sudden rage which made his body tremble. He had bumped into a butcher's trolley which was being unloaded on the street. His shirt was stained with streaks of blood and he had thrown it away before catching the plane back to India. He never wanted to see his son again and for some strange reason Mala never asked him about his visit. Anyway even if she had asked he would have had nothing to say. He had wiped the memory of his son, the country that had made him into a common shopkeeper, a clown who danced and joked to amuse his clientele of old women.

This farm with its twenty acres of black, rich soil where the best wheat grew, this house and the money in the bank would last his lifetime and then he did not care who got it after he died. Mala had never been interested in farming and when they came here after he retired from his duties as a judge, she had seemed very quiet but she had never said anything to him and he assumed she liked being here just as much as he did. He went in to Chandigarh, a town nearby, three days a week to advise a law firm on difficult cases and the rest of the time he read his law books and made notes. He was planning to write a book on criminal law which students of the evening law school could use.

He liked to help students, especially bright and poor ones because they were always so grateful. It was a pleasant feeling to have young boys bow and touch his feet when he walked into a room. In winter he often gave a lift in his car to one or two law students who hung around their office, hoping to get some work. But he made sure they sat in front with the driver and he only exchanged a few words with them during the entire journey which lasted an hour. There was no need to be too friendly with them, they might mistake it for weakness or even loneliness in him and that would be terrible since he had nothing even remotely to do with anything like that.

Sometimes when he came home late in the evenings from town he would see Mala roaming about behind the house and as the car headlights caught her slender figure, lit up her face, he was always surprised to see how beautiful she was still. She did not seem so beautiful when he had seen her for the first time in her father's house, dressed in a simple cotton sari with white flowers in her hair. He had recently seen those flowers somewhere in the garden. Jog looked around the room to see where the butterflies had settled but could not find them anywhere. Their black and white wings had merged with the curtains and now they could live here safely for ever. Mala would have liked that. What did she really like? He knew she liked this room which was the smallest in the house with windows that looked out into the garden. The ceiling was made of wood unlike the rest of the house and the floor was a deep red colour which shone even at night. Mala had moved into this room soon after they came to live on the farm. "I like it here. It is so cosy and friendly," she had said.

Was she lonely here? Her family lived in a crowded area of Delhi where you could not even take the smallest car in. His mother had grumbled about walking through the narrow lane to meet Mala's family, holding a handkerchief to her nose, but his father had insisted on the match. "Her father is a very learned man. They are a decent family. The girl will make a good wife for Jog."

Mala's brothers and their wives talked loudly and argued endlessly sitting around their tiny dining table, the men in their vests. They drank sweet strong tea which their mother brewed in a dark kitchen. Jog got a headache each time he had to visit them which thankfully was very seldom since Mala was often ill and could not travel. There was no question of having them to stay – not that Mala had ever asked. Though one night she had called out for her mother but when Jog had asked her what she wanted she had kept quiet.

Now he would not have to see them ever again. They had come for the funeral and had left immediately. Jog felt a sudden emptiness in the house as if many people had lived here and had suddenly gone away. The ceiling seemed too high, the walls too white. There were so many empty rooms where people seem to whisper all day long. Mala's bed had a clean white sheet on it but someone had rested their head on her pillow, he could see the hollow filled with blue shadows. Had he slept here last night? Jog could not remember. As he turned to go, the butterfly came out and flew out of the open window.

Jog walked out into the verandah that circled the house. Raman used to rollerskate round and round, singing at the top of his voice till Jog had put a stop to it. The skates made a terrible screeching sound which grated on his nerves and the floor got scratched with white lines. Mala had kept all irritating sounds away from him, forming a safe barrier around him. No hawkers ever came to the house while he was there, the servants hid behind doors and even the birds called in soft tones in the garden while he was at home. Mala had seen to it. She stood like a loyal, silent sentry guarding his temper, shielding his moods and now he felt a sudden anger surge through him. She had no business to die and leave him to deal with the world. Most of the time he was left alone in the house; the servants, well trained by her, cooked, cleaned and vanished out of sight when he was at home. He was hardly aware of their existence except when he saw their hands as they gave him his cup of tea or handed him a letter or took money from him.

Jog looked out at the lawns which now were turning brown in the heat. The rains were about to come but though the sky turned dark each morning, the clouds floated away by the time the sun had set, leaving a moist heaviness in the air. Mala had managed to keep the lawn green even in summer by diverting the water from the kitchen into the garden. She had asked him if mali could hire some extra labour to do it and though he had not really been listening to what she was saying, he had said yes. Now he could understand what she had been saying. The narrow channel, edged with pebbles, ran along the verandah and opened out into the lawns and then flowed down to the flower beds beyond. Jog could hear the water gurgling and followed the sound to see where it led. He should have changed his slippers but the sound of the flowing water seemed to call him urgently. The shade of the mango trees fell on his eyes and he had to blink to adjust to the dim light. A sudden splash of bright red surprised him, the tomatoes, hanging from the green stems, looked almost artificial amidst all the dry grass.

As he came out of the shade of the mango tree, a green and gold patchwork quilt of plants spread out before him and he stopped to inhale the sharp, fresh scent. At first he was not sure what these green plants were, they all seemed to look alike except some had yellow leaves but when he went closer he could see chillies hanging like long green nails, purple aubergines, heavy with seed, green tomatoes and tiny cucumbers with white dots on them. He walked through them, the wet mud staining his shoes and he could feel the warm earth on his tongue. A creeper trailed along the path, scattering yellow flowers and then he saw a huge green pumpkin half-eaten by ants. He bent down to see if there were any more pumpkins hiding under the leaves when a thin dog with a black patch on its eye came out of the bushes and lay down at his feet, wagging its stumpy tail as if he knew him. They had never kept a dog in the house. Jog did not like the way their canine smell took over the entire house, especially when they were old and sick. "Bibiji used to feed him. He keeps looking for her...What is written by the gods we have to accept," said Mali rising up from the flowerbed. "She gave him biscuits, bread, now he won't eat my chappatis. She taught him to chase the crows away from the flower beds, gave him a biscuit each time he did it. Though she never allowed him to catch one." Jog looked down at the dog, rolling in the dust at his feet. He did not know Mala had liked dogs. They could have kept one – a good highly pedigreed Alsation. Many of his fellow judges kept guard dogs to scare away trouble-makers from the courts.

Mali had gathered a basketful of tomatoes. "I was just bringing these into the house. Bibiji had planted all these seedlings just before she went away," said the old man, wiping a tear from his eyes. How easy it was for this wily, uneducated man to cry. He must be planning to sell the tomatoes. Probably sold all the fruit and vegetables from our garden. I am going to keep an eye on him. When did she have time to plant all these flowers? Jog touched the plants gently with his hands as he walked down the garden, the dog running after him. A flock of crows flew past them and the dog suddenly went mad barking and leaping around the plants. "Stop, don't trample the flowers," said Jog and the dog sat down at once, panting heavily, his dark eyes full of happiness. "She called him 'Daku'," said Mali and suddenly Jog felt very irritated that the old man should know so much about Mala. "Go and do your work. From tomorrow you must bring all the flowers and vegetables into the house. I will check them all," he said as Mali nodded and hurriedly moved back a few steps.

So this is where all the mogras in her hair came from. She always wore fresh flowers in her hair but when she fell ill, she just kept a bowl of buds by her bed. The nurse was not very happy about it but Mala pleaded with her to keep the flowers. "Please, they make me feel I am still alive," he had heard her say one day. That seemed many years ago. Her voice was fading from his memory now and Jog felt a sudden finger of fear touch his heart. He would forget her face too very soon, her skin which had been like silk under his touch, her fragrance. The mind would not hold her. Jog walked aimlessly through the garden, his clothes tinged with pollen and dirt. He came to a makeshift wooden bridge and then stepped into a circular patch.

Mogra flowers grew on every shrub, even the ones that were hardly a foot high from the ground and butterflies sat in close groups on the white flowers.They were yellow with orange tips on the edge of their wings, very different from the ones that had flown into Mala's bedroom, Jog laughed as he tried to remember the pattern on their wings. "She would have found it so strange if I had ever asked her what colour a butterfly's wing was." He wandered down to the grove of guava trees but the scent of the mogra flowers seemed to grow stronger as he walked away. Mala's face rose before him, her soft brown eyes smiled as she tucked a garland of mogra flowers in her hair. Had I ever seen her doing that? Sometimes a garland lay near her bed but I never saw her actually putting the flowers in her hair. All he could remember was that she always carried a faint pleasant perfume wherever she went in the house but it was only now as he stood in this garden that he realized these were the flowers she wore in her hair.

The next day Jog woke up at dawn. Mali, surprised to see him in the garden, dropped his cup of tea and leapt up. Daku ran around him and then suddenly stopped when Jog reached into his pocket to take out a packet of biscuits. He unwrapped the cover, took out one biscuit then folded the packet neatly before putting it back in his pocket. Daku watched him, his dark eyes worried yet happy with anticipation. "You will get only one biscuit, my boy. Understand? Just one," Jog said. Mali was pulling a plastic pipe out from under his charpoy. "Bibiji liked to water the seedling herself. The water channel never had enough water in summer. So we dug this tube-well. I mean Sahib had it done. I told her so many times, you will get your hands dirty. So much mud here. But she just laughed. 'Baba, I had to water twenty-five flower pots in my house. My father had made it my duty. We brothers and sisters all had different duties to do around the house. Mine was to be a mali like you,' she used to say." Jog looked at the heavy water pipe. How could her slender hands have carried this heavy thing? He could not imagine her watering the garden, playing with the dog, chatting about her family to this old man. Yet she must have spend all her time here while he was away at work, tending to these plants, planning what seeds to sow, where to grow vegetables and how to divide the flower beds so that they got the maximum sunlight. She must have discussed all this with Mali, asked his advice, let him help her with the heavy tasks. A stab of jealousy hit him in his stomach. Jog wanted to shake the old man, to snatch all the memories he had of Mala in his head. He desperately wanted to ask Mali so many things about her but he could not speak.

Jog pulled the waterpipe across the chilli patch, taking care not to touch the plants and then let the water run into the tomato plants. For a minute the water stopped and then gushed out with force, creating a furrow in the earth. A sweet fragrance of wet earth rose as the water ran around the plants and slowly soaked into the ground. He stood very still, Daku sat next to him, his thin body pressed warmly against his leg. The sky was clear with just a streak of white feathery clouds, like it had been the day Mala died.

The tears came slowly, washing his face, yet he could not feel their wetness as his hands touched the seedlings she had planted. He was afraid to hurt them and let the water wash the dust from them, gently, one leaf at a time.

The mustard fields shone in the late afternoon light and the crows had flown away to the river bank now. The house rested. All the twenty-six guests had been fed and their servants too had eaten well. They had all praised the food, especially the cauliflower and the mango chutney. They thanked Badibua one by one, took an extra betel leaf for the journey and left. When they were outside the gates, past the mustard fields, one of them remarked there had been too much salt in the dal. The others agreed. But they all thought that Badibua had conducted herself well. She did not show off her new found wealth neither was she stingy with her money and had given them all a good feast. "Must have done a lot of good in her last life to have got this house, all these fertile fields and four faithful servants too. When the Lord gives, the roofs shatter with his generosity" said one elderly woman spitting the betel nuts on the path.

All the windows were shut to keep the afternoon sun out. Badibua dozed, her eyes half-closed. Malarani was curled up on the other bed, Sharada and Nanni on durries on the floor with pillows tucked under their heads. The feast had gone off well. None had complained or quarelled with each other. The food had not run short though they could have made another cauldron of mango chutney. Well, you could never have enough of mango chutney, however much you made it always ran short. It was a rule of life, thought Badibua and sighed.

Malarani heard her sigh but she knew it was a contented sigh which did not need a reply and went back to sleep. Badibua had asked her to come and live with her, to help her with the farm. What two women, well past fifty, could do she did not know but she was happy to try. It would be a relief to live here away from the nagging relatives. Badibua would give her a permanent home, she was sure, a place she could die in happily.

Shashi and Choni sat on the swing in the verandah and chatted aimlessly while Hema wiped the silverware with an old cloth. They heard the older women's gentle snores float out into the verandah and laughed. They had decided to stay a few days longer and help Badibua with the mustard harvest. "I have never seen mustard being harvested though," said Choni. Hema looked up and said. "I know how it is done. You just hold the seed pods against the wind. We used to do it in my village."

Soon the women would wake up and Hema went in to prepare tea for them. She would add ginger and seeds of cardamom. The women had worked so hard, they deserved a good cup of sweet, strong tea. Maybe there was still time for one more story before the sun set. That is if the women had not dreamt away the story. "After all dreams too are stories our heart tells us," thought Hema as she crushed the seeds of cardamom.

Eight

I think of all our duties, the duty to our dead ancestors are the most difficult. Escpecially the women. They are never happy with what we do. The men are pleased with a few well cooked dishes, a nice milky sweet but the women...they are another story. Sharada had so much trouble with her mother-in-law, I remember. The women had heard Sharada's tale last year but they did not mind hearing it again. She always added a few new details to the story and anyway they had forgotten some bits since there were so many people involved – all these brothers and sisters who lived in various corners of the world they had never heard of.

SHARADA'S STORY

When they left for the airport, to fetch the second lot of relatives arriving on the British Airways flight, her face was already tired of smiling. The week stretched ahead like a long, unfamiliar road full of hidden pitfalls. It was not as if Sharada disliked her husband's family, in fact she was quite fond of some of them, especially when they brought her expensive gifts and confided in her about each other's faults, but this morning she was anxious. The thought of having all seven of them together, bubbling and simmering like a rich, oily curry...spilling into every corner of her home and staining it, worried her so much that she began to have nightmares. Even before the first lot arrived at the crack of dawn, she had began seeing them in her dreams, squabbling and spitting venom at each other. When she woke up in the morning she was confused about what had happened and what was about to happen.

They were flying in from different parts of the world like migratory birds, dragging reluctant husbands and sullen children to take part in their late mother's annual shraad ceremony. She had been dead for two years so the loss was diffused by time but the emotional outpouring still retained its power and joy especially when they were all together in their late mother's living room, sitting on the sofa she had chosen, reclining on cushions she had embroidered. Now that the shock and grief had passed, they found it quite enjoyable to sit around the dining table, their hands still fragrant with rich curry, chewing pieces of fish bones and lamenting over their dead mother. The sons would sob with dignity while the daughters would dab their eyes delicately with their napkins and then ask her if the colour ran – one never knew with these Indian handlooms!

Sharada tried to forget the trauma of last winter and tuned her mind to cope with the new worries that lay ahead. The road to the airport seemed longer than ever. She wished the old lady had died in summer because these NRIs were terrified of power cuts, water shortages, eye, skin and stomach infections which they knew summer brought. But the old lady, with an uncanny sense of timing, had died in the middle of a perfect winter afternoon so that her sons and daughters spread all over the world could fly home each year to pay their respects. Sharada wondered what would have happened if Vinod too had flown to another country like the rest of them. But he had not and now it was their responsibility to hold the shraad ceremony each year. It was, thankfully, a simple ceremony with a short havan pooja followed by a lunch just for the family. But before it happened, she had to deal with the chaos of all the emotional drama that would lead up to the final day.

Sharada tried to soothe her mind by playing her favourite game. The shraad ceremony was over and done with, everyone had flown back to their various homes in distant lands, the week ahead was now just a confused, half-forgotten memory which she could rummage through sometimes, before falling asleep at night.

There were five different kinds of curry on the table, the bright red colour fading to pale orange according to the strength of chillies. The old steel bowl, gleaming like burnished silver since it had been scrubbed clean with a new dishwashing liquid Ashok had got from the U.S., held the very hot, deep red curry for those who lived here, that meant just Sharada, Vinod, Bejon and Masi. Next to it sat the quiet, red, medium hot curry for those who visited India more than once a year and though they had chilli-proof stomachs they still had to be cautious, which meant only Ashok. Then there was a mild, faded red, watery curry for those who came to India only once a year and whose stomachs knew how to deal with curry but were not totally chilli-proof. This mild yet delicious curry was also for those who had over indulged at the last meal and needed to soothe their agitated stomachs. This included both residents and visiting relatives. By the end of the NRI visit this medium red curry would become the most favourite one. Then at the end of the table, simmering quietly in a transparent white bone china bowl, was a pale pink, bland "sick-man's" curry for those who had just got off the plane and needed to be gently reminded about the magic of Indian curry which their stomachs, full of pasta, burgers and roast chicken, had forgotten about. Finally, in a bunny rabbit bowl, there was a stew-curry for the NRI children who were frightened of spices, turning bright red with the lashings of tomato ketchup they had poured in it to make the whole thing more palatable.

Though Sharada had placed the curries in the correct order, the dishes had got mixed up and there was a confusion of red, orange and pink on the dining table. Masi, the oldest surviving relative with an intact mind, who had just arrived from Ambala, had served herself the "sick man's curry" and the lines on her thin face grew deeper as she grimaced, putting the spoon down. "What is this dish water, Sharada? Take it away at once! My dear departed sister would have been shocked to see this kind of hospital food on her dining table," she said, wiping her hands on the table cloth. Luckily it was orange and the curry stains would not show.

"That is for Ashok Bhaiya, he wanted light food till his stomach could get used to the spices," said Sharada, placing the pale curry in front of Ashok from Seattle, who had already taken a spoonful of the deep red, very hot curry and was looking at her in alarm. "Yes.... Remember last time how he got the runs and had to sit near the exit door on the train when we went to Agra?" said Bejon, the eldest brother, and a resident who had never left the country except during the second world war briefly for a short visit to London to sell his collection of old coins for a fortune. He helped himself to the rich red gravy, the sight of which made Ashok blanch. He took a gelusil tablet out of his shirt pocket and placed it next to his plate, as if to ward off the aroma of spices that floated down from Bejon's aromatic curry to his pale golden one. "You NRIs always have weak stomachs. Look at me. I am going to be seventy next month, yet I can have a full plate of Moti Mahal butter chicken without any problem," said Bejon, his mouth full of chicken curry.

"The problem is ours when you burp and fart all over the place," muttered Ashok.

"What, what was that...?" said Bejon, jutting out his curry red chin.

"There is chana paishe after this," said Sharada quickly to defuse the tension.

"How did you make it? With fresh paneer, I hope! I always make it with fresh paneer, made with whey. Nothing else tastes as good," said Masi, getting up from the table though the others were still eating. As soon as she reached the kitchen door, Jaya from Manchester said, "That is the fuddy duddy old way to make 'paishe'. I just dump leftover sweets into boiling milk." Masi stood still at the door, her back to them. Then she turned slowly and pointed one yellow turmeric stained finger at Jaya. "Do not speak like an idiot. My dead sister always said you were the most foolish of her seven children – may god take care of the two dead ones," Masi said, coming back to the dining table. "To make a perfect chana paishe you have to make fresh cottage cheese with whey – not lemon. And not this foul thing called vinegar which you people abroad pour into every dish," she said fixing each one of them, even Bejon, who had never tasted vinegar, with an angry look. And then when her outburst went unchallenged, she left the room. They could hear her rubber slippers flip flop down the corridor. Soon afterwards, when there was silence, Jaya from Manchester spoke again but in a soft voice. "Who has the time to make fresh whey and whatnot. Just throw all the leftover sweets into a pot of boiling milk and you have a dreamy channa paishe. You should serve this tomorrow Sharada, there will be so many boxes of leftover sweets." Suddenly, silently without warning, Masi was amidst them again, her thin white-clad figure shimmering at the head of the table like Banquo's ghost. "You

will not make that horrible dish fit only for servants at my poor
dead sister's shraad. I will not allow it till there is breath in my
old body. I will make the paishe and I alone will serve it to the
priest. I want my sister's spirit to be at peace. Imagine crossing
the river of death with a plateful of foreign pish pash, a paishe
made with rotting sweets, served as an offering to the guardian
of death. Never ... never," Masi hissed, wiping a tear from her
eye. Ashok Seattle began to sniffle at once and his sisters followed
in order of age. First Jaya Manchester began to sob, then Bonti
New Jersey, Babi Berlin and Choti London joined with a low wail
and from behind came a deep bass sound as Bejon India burped.
"Bless the old lady," he said as the children tried to stifle their
nervous giggles. They had only seen emotional outpourings like
this on television and were not sure how to react. Should they
join in like an invited studio audience or sit back and watch like
passive viewers? Their parents were of no help, in fact ever since
they had landed in India they had changed into alien beings who
sang, laughed, shouted and cried like strangers! They had been
warned about the way things were at home, how they should
beware of oddballs and never take sweets or a lift from them.

"She likes my channa paishe" said Jaya Manchester looking at
Masi Ambala defiantly. "She told me herself during Bonti's son's
thread ceremony."

"Did she really? I thought she had stopped talking to you
after you threw Baba's portrait into the garage along with the
old suitcases during one of your cleaning dramas...." said Babi
Toronto, getting up from the table. Jaya gave her an angry look
but did not retort since she wanted to deal with Masi first. She
would settle with Babi later. There were many thing to sort out.
The old diamond and ruby necklace that Ma had given her to
reset, a friend visiting Toronto had seen Babi wearing it though

she claimed it was lost. Jaya faced Masi, her chin pointing up uncannily like Masi's. "I cannot recall her exact words but she did say to me before we stopped talking, 'Jaya I like the fast way you cook sweets'."

"She never ate sweets! Only I know how she hated sweet things! 'Sister, save me from these horrible home-made sweets my wretched daughter makes,' she used to say. One day she went off with the driver and ayah to have sambar idli to take away the taste of some foul English rice pudding you had forced her to eat," said Masi standing close to the table, her curry-stained hand resting on the back of Ashok's chair. He shifted, his face twitching as the smell of stale curry stung his delicate nose. He hoped she would not touch his head. Masi twitched too. She needed to go to the bathroom urgently but she could not leave the table at such a crucial stage when anything could be said against her poor dead sister. Masi had to hold on to her bladder, pressing her thin thighs together, to save the family honour. Her father had been a Raibahadur and he had taught them never to allow anyone to say a single word against the Tripathi clan. She had never really liked her sister, god rest her soul, but now that she was dead and not here to speak for herself, who could defend her except for her sole surviving sister? She was the only one left in the clan now who remembered their former glory and fame. The horse and buggy at the door, the uniformed servants, the English guests around this very teak dining table. Her mother had given it to her sister though she had asked for it. It would have fitted in so well in her huge dining room. She would have had the chairs reupholstered in velvet. Anyway what is gone is gone. Her sister was in heaven now and she was here alive, fighting fit and at the dining table to defend their family name.

"Channa paishe with stale leftover sweets!" A shudder of

horror ran down Masi's fragile frame and for the first time she felt happy she did not have a brood of idiotic children. Just one son who lived peacefully with her, who did not even have a passport, who would never allow his wife – a dark but well-behaved girl – to speak in front of her elders. Her sister had spoiled her children, especially the daughters, made them into brown mems and now she had to deal with them.

"I never forced her to eat anything. Anyway I cannot believe Ma ever ate out. She told me 'I hate eating food that has not been cooked in my kitchen, by my own cook, in front of my eyes,'" said Babi though Masi was attacking Jaya. This was a signal that the fight was now open. Immediately everyone joined the fray!

Ashok jumped in first. "What nonsense you talk Babi. Ma came with Sandra and me to the Bukhara each time we were here. She loved tandoori fish," he said, moving his chair closer to the table, to be safe from Masi in case she began waving her arms about. Bejon, who was taking a catnap, woke up with a start when he heard tandoori fish and then, when he saw there was none on the table, fell asleep again, his head resting on his chest.

"What nonsense! You know Ma never ate meat. She became a vegetarian after she visited Badrinath. We never even cooked meat at home when she came to stay with us. The smell made her sick she said and we had to open all the windows even though it was freezing outside," Babi said. Jaya suddenly wanted to help her sister.

"Maybe she ate non-veg because of Sandra being there. You know Ma wanted her to feel at home though she was so unhappy when you married a white girl. First one to do that in our family," Jaya said this softly so that Bejon would not wake up and take the last piece of prawn which she had her eye on.

"She was not unhappy. She loved Sandra and just before she died she sent her a Christmas card. She wrote a note in it saying 'You are a good girl even though you are a foreigner. I will leave my heavy gold necklace with emeralds for you,'" said Ashok. "Of course, we never saw it."

Jaya was about to help herself to the prawn but her hand froze and Babi seized the opportunity and picked it up quickly. "Her heavy gold necklace. What are you saying Askok Bhaiya. She gave them to Baby when she got engaged. You were there Masi when she put it around her neck with her own hands. We had come to India that year to buy saris." Masi did not reply. She was not going to help Jaya out so quickly. Setting her lips in a firm line, she picked up a guava and began to peel it. This helped to take her mind off the bathroom. Everyone watched her as she cut the fruit in five segments and then when she offered the first one to Ashok. Jaya wished she had not confronted Masi with the Channa paishe but how did she know that Ashok would bring up the gold bangle issue. That was a very serious topic, kept on hold for late night after-dinner discussions and never aired so casually at the lunch table, certainly not when outsiders were around. All the sons-in-law and daughters-in-law though they had been married for at least twenty years were still considered outsiders and no real family discussions about gold or property ever took place when they were around. It was an unspoken rule and now Ashok had broken it! Just as well that Sandra woman was not at the dining table. The food on the plane had knocked her out and now she lay asleep in Ma's bedroom, with a lavender soaked handkerchief on her eyes.

Sharada, her neck tight with tension, tried to get everyone to talk about what they would have for dinner. That usually helped to clear the air of old conflicts and bring in a fresh war cry since each one demanded a different dish which the other thought was terrible for their health or tastebuds. Then Masi spoke suddenly, "My poor dead sister told me just before she left us that Ashok has brought shame into the family by marrying a white girl." The wave of silence that swept over the dining table was so overwhelming that even the servants helping themselves to the leftover food in the pots and pans in the kitchen were touched by it and their hands froze in midair as they waited for someone to break the silence. Sharada hoped Sandra was still weak and would not come down.

"She said that? She told you that about me?"Ashok said, taking his glasses off and rubbing his eyes as if he suddenly could not recognize Masi anymore and needed to see who she was more clearly.

Masi realized she had gone too far and shrugged her shoulders. She offered another piece of guava to Ashok who took it, feeling its edges like a blind man before putting it in his mouth. They heard him bite the seeds. In the kitchen the servant began to bang the dishes noisily once more. They were waiting for the family to finish so that they could clear the table and then sit down to eat. A rich red curry, the sixth and the strongest one, hissed angrily on the fire for them. Bejon snored gently.

"Masi, I don't think Ma could have said such a thing. She did not mind when I married Chong though he was half American. Ma was way ahead of her time though she was not educated, and she had a lot of instinctive intelligence. She was not an old wife like most other women of her generation," said Bonti speaking quickly before Masi could fix her piercing gaze on her. Ashok looked at his youngest sister with gratitude. He never thought she was so brave and would come to his rescue. If only she had not married that funny Chinese American he would have liked to visit her more often. There was a cheap flight to New Jersey from Seattle. But the thought of Chong and his yellow face made him nervous. Her house smelt like a Chinese takeaway and though Sandra liked them, he could not get used to having a Chinese brother-in-law. Why did she not choose a decent white man? She was a good looking woman. How could anyone marry a Chinese?

"Ma did not say anything about your half-caste husband who is neither a white man or a black or brown one! She did not talk about you at all. All she said once was that you should lose weight or else that Chingchong-chinaman would divorce you one day soon," said Masi who now knew for sure that her position as the last person to have spoken to the departed soul was undisputed by all the other family members. Sharada was the only one who had met the old lady before she sank into a year long senile dementia which had gradually floated her into a coma. But Sharada was an outsider and did not matter. Sandra the other outsider mattered even less since she was white. Very sensible and thoughtful of her to have fallen ill.

"Ma never bothered about my weight. She always said 'eat more, eat more, you look weak.' In fact she told me Jaya's the one who should watch out," said Bonti, not looking at her older sister. Jaya, who was feeling relieved about Masi not crossing over to the enemy side as far as the gold necklace was concerned, was taken aback by this unfair barb from her sister to whom she had just this very morning given a pure silk sari – a new one which Sharada had given her last winter for Diwali but which she had not worn since it was blue and Sharada knew very well that she hated blue. Anyway she never wore saris at home. Dressed in pants and jackets she passed off as one of the tribe.

No one ever thought of her as Indian at the store. A blue silk sari would make her stand out like a sore thumb. Jaya longed for her quiet, flower filled home in the suburbs of Manchester. A week more to go. She tried to come up with something to hit back with but all that she could think of was bathing Bonti once when she had chicken-pox. Ma had told her to put lukewarm water but Jaya had poured hot water by mistake and Bonti had cried for an hour trying to tell Ma what Jaya had done but Ma had scolded her for being a crybaby for nothing. Ma did love her. In her own way she loved all of them though they were never sure what that way was. "Ma liked plump women. She was thin herself but she said women should have some padding or their husbands run away," said Jaya though she knew this was a feeble rejoinder. Bonti suddenly looked at her and smiled. Jaya took a little bit of chutney, placed it on a small piece of guava and put it in Bonti's mouth. They laughed like two little girls caught in a naughty game.

Sharada thought this was a good time to get up from the table and tried to get Masi into the kitchen by waving a red flag. "Please, could you see if the servants have finished all the rice?" Bejon could be left at the table, he was fast asleep and Babi had gone into the kitchen. But just then Ashok Bhaiya spoke, "When your husband died Ma said he was all alone with only a servant. You had gone out to play cards with your neighbour." No one was quite sure who this remark was meant for since there were two women with dead husbands around the table and both played rummy. When nobody responded to this, it flew around the table and then sank on the ground where the paper napkins lay crumpled. Ashok Bhaiya decided to be more direct. He looked at Jaya who was his actual target and not Masi who was a witness. "America has made her a bad wife, Ma wrote to me

once. I may still have the letter....I have heard Jaya plays cards
all day while her poor husband cooks and cleans. All my training
gone to waste. One daughter a card sharpie and the other a slow
lazy slob," Ashok's voice rose in a whine that sounded like an old
woman's voice.

"She could never have said such a cruel thing about us,"
muttered Bonti, "I know I am slow but Ma said I was methodical.
She hated anyone doing anything quickly. You remember how
she slapped you one day when you wore your nighty inside out
at night to save time folding it the right way in the morning?"
she asked her sister Choti from London who was trying to
scrape the last bit of mild curry from the dish and had not taken
part in the conversation till now since she had a painfully sore
throat and could only grunt. But now, her voice cracked and
hoarse, burst out like a series of rapid gun shots. "No, I don't
remember. You are talking rubbish. Ma never hit any of us. She
was the kindest, gentlest soul that ever lived," said Choti with
a long sigh and everyone waited – tears on hold – to see if she
would cry. Mild sniffles were allowed but real tears were kept on
hold for the evening post-dinner sessions but sometimes, if the
situation demanded it, one could sob during lunch. But Choti,
her eyes puffed up with jet-lag, only cleared her throat and
then she began to mix a spoonful of rice with the gravy she had
salvaged. Then there was only the sound of her chewing. Vinod,
who had also kept out of the conversation since, had been busy
talking on his cell-phone throughout lunch, decided to sing an
old song which had been his mother's favourite. "Mere piya gaye
Rangoon,wahan say kiya hai telephoon..thumari yaad satati hai,
jiya may aag lagati hai ..." (My love has gone to Rangoon, from
where he telephoned, saying he missed me, his heart burned for
me) he sang as if to lull his older siblings to sleep. The servants

sighed in the kitchen as they quietly helped themselves to small handfuls of rice and curry. They should have waited till the table was cleared but the sun had already travelled far beyond the roof and soon they would be demanding tea and god knows what.

The others began to hum along with Vinod and those who had forgotten the words of the song helped themselves to whatever bits of food were left at the bottom of the dishes. As their lazy fingers salvaged bits of curry their dead mother's face floated past them, her white hair streaming behind her like a silver shadow. She looked down at them, her sharp gaze broken into fragments by the afternoon light. Each one thought only they had seen her so they kept quiet, their hearts fluttering with fear and joy. She hovered quite close to them, her white eyes glittering over the remnants of food on the dining table, the curry stained tablecloth, her assorted family. Her hands touched each one of them briefly, lingering over Bejan, her first born, longer than the rest. He raised his eyes, dull with sleep and food, but she rose in the air, scattering her gentle touch into tiny pieces. So she remained, curving, encircling, arching and floating over them for a long time but the fragmented image she gave to her family gathered around the table could not join into a whole. They tried but could not hold her, feel her gentle, unfamiliar touch, she had never caressed them as children and they were hungry for her touch. They lifted their hands to catch her but there was only a shaft of silver light, shiny with dust. Then as the afternoon faded into dusk, she went away, gliding over the trees and the servants came in to clear the table.

Nine

"Duty is the most important thing to remember all your life. Duty to your dead ancestors, your father, your husband and then your son, and if you are fortunate, your grandson. It is the women who fulfil their duty without complaining, without even thinking they are doing it..." said Badibua.

"Yes, I too did my duty," whispered Nanni. The women were surprised to hear her voice because she hardly ever spoke. Was she going to tell her story today? They waited. Almost all the vegetables had been done, the rice cleaned, and as soon as Badibua gave the signal, they would start the cooking. Nanni would have to be quick with her story or else wait till next year. Just as they were fretting about this, Nanni obliged.

NANNI'S STORY

The first day Nanni had to cook was when she was a three-day old bride with henna still dark and fragrant on her palms. She was sitting on the bridal bed, her head aching with the scent of rose petals which lay scattered all over the bed sheets, the pillows and the floor. A few stray petals, curling at the edges like pink claws, clung to her hair and when she tried to remove them her heavy gold pins – the ones her mother had tied her hair with – pierced her head and she began to cry. Home suddenly seemed so far away yet she could hear her mother's voice as she shouted at the servants to get the food ready for the wedding feast as she put the golden pins in her hair one by one, grumbling about how much they had cost. "But let them see we are not paupers like them," she had hissed, the pins clenched between her teeth. In this house where her mother said she would have to live till she died, there was just one old servant. She was still brushing off the rose petals when he had come into the corridor outside her room and coughed. "What is it?" she had asked finally after he had coughed and cleared his throat many times, because she was not sure whether she was supposed to speak at all and that too to a male servant. "Bhabhi has fallen ill. Dada is asking if you can cook something or should he ask someone to come from the village." Nanni, her head dizzy with the perfume of stale roses, took the decision that was to ruin her life for ever.

She got up, tripped over her heavy bridal sari, and said in a clear 16-year old voice. "I will make the food today. Tell Bhabhi to rest." Then she took off her sari, folding it carefully like her mother had shown her. Most of her jewellery had already been taken off by Bhabhi and locked up in a tin trunk, with a curt "I am keeping them safe for you, tell your mother." She took off the remaining chains and two heavy bangles and hid them under the mattress. She knew she had to keep her mangalsutra necklace, her nose ring and six toe rings on as long as her husband was alive. Then she quickly dressed in a plain cotton sari, a pink one with yellow flowers, pulled the palla over her face and opened the door. There was no one outside so she uncovered her face fully and looked around. There were two doors on either side of her room but both were locked with big padlocks. She could hear someone snoring, the sound was coming at regular intervals through a half open door at the end of the corridor. She decided to go towards it.

The kitchen was a dark hollow with a tiny window covered with a red curtain that made everything look darker that it was. The mustard oil jars lined up on the shelf gleamed like blood, the onions had a strange pink colour and the white marble chakla too looked as if they had pounded meat on it. A brick stove stood in one corner, the embers were just about to die out. Nanni pulled out a few pieces of wood from a pile next to the window and as she fed the dying fire she saw through tear-filled eyes her mother's kitchen at home. The gleaming floor which was polished with coconut fibres every morning, the brass vessels that shone like gold and the line of 30 glass jars each filled with a special pickle. Her father refused to eat the same pickle everyday so her mother gave him a new one, every day for thirty days and then repeated the cycle because he had forgotten what he had had by then.

"We were never good enough for them," her husband said as he chewed the bones with his eyes shut. She hated the way he talked and ate at the same time, his words always slurring with curry and malice against her family. His hatred for her, crushing, mingling with his saliva, poured into the food she had cooked for him. She had not minded at first because her mother had told her to be quiet and well-behaved all the time, however aggravating the situation may be. "Remember you are our daughter. Raja Dinkar's granddaughter. Do not bring shame on us." She had sat silently through hundreds of meals, listening to her husband berating her family, each meal would bring out a new dislike, a fresh grudge he held against her father, her mother or her brothers. So many years had passed, both her parents were dead, her brother had renounced the world and become a sadhu yet Harish would not let go. Like a rabid dog he kept yapping at them, chasing their memory, recalling each word they had said to him, digging out hidden insults. When his mother had been alive, she would join in too and together they would eat and spit venom at her. She had a sharper tongue and sharper memory and could even say on which date at what hour her father had let them down. "Remember," she would say, wagging a finger stained with food, "remember the day your uncle got married, it was when the wheat crop had failed on our farm, the day you got chicken pox. It was at lunchtime that the great sahib arrived. Just a box of sweets, plain burfee. No money, no clothes, nothing. The mean goat. What was he going to do with all his money, I asked him. Has he taken it with him? Has he? Has he?" she would say, jutting her chin out at Nanni and pointing for another serving of dal.

That first day when she had cooked, twenty years ago, she should have poisoned them all. His mother, father, brother-in-law, uncle, and him. But she had been young and foolish and wanted so much to please them all. Her mother had been a great cook and she wanted to show them how well she had been taught by her. She wanted to manage the house, look after the old people and most of all she wanted her husband to love her. That first meal she had cooked, her eyes blind with tears from the smoke, her hands shaking with fear, had stunned them. "You little sparrow. How did you cook so much?" her husband said later when they were alone. The rose petals now suddenly seemed fragrant as they lay together sharing the same pillow. They had been so pleased with her cooking that day that for the next twenty years she was sent to the kitchen to do all the cooking. "A wife's first duty is to feed her husband well," they said to her as the entire family, thirteen of them, sat down to eat. She got up at dawn, coaxed the kitchen fire into life, ground the spices and began the first meal of the day. The old servant felt sorry for her and tried to help but her mother-in-law would not let him touch the food. "I have been cooking for the family for thirty years and now it is your turn. Do not think you are a princess just because your father claims to be so rich. All lies. We have yet to see the colour of his money in this house."

The old lady had died five years ago, keeling over at a wedding feast after eating three bowls of kheer. "She went straight to her maker, a short, sweet death," said the neighbour in whose house the feast had been held. Harish did not seem as distraught as she thought he would be without his beloved mother, who had never left his side from the day he had been born –a breech baby with a head full of black hair. She slept next to them all throughout their married life and the only time they had been alone had been a few days after her wedding. Then after that the old lady had moved her bed into their room, thrust her bundle of saris into Nanni's dowry chest. Her father-in-law had been alive then but he stayed out most nights. Nanni had heard the aunts whispering about another wife somewhere in a village beyond the hills. When Harish wanted to make love to her, he would touch her with a pillow and they would tip-toe to the other room. She had loved the secrecy and Harish had seemed so romantic during their stealthy, hurried but urgent lovemaking. Later during the day he would come and stand near the kitchen door and watch her as she cooked. They spoke in whispers and laughed with their hands on their mouths. But that was such a long time ago. Harish was a different man then with another face, another voice. Now she hated his touch and even wished his mother were alive for then he would not spend hours smothering her in their bed, his weak helpless body trying and failing to make love to her.

Though now they had two servants, Harish would not eat if she did not cook the food. "You cannot let them touch the food. I will die if I have to eat food cooked by those two dirty scoundrels. I would throw them out if I could walk to the door," he screamed each time Nanni let one of the servants into the kitchen. "I am shackled and bound to the kitchen. He will not even have tea made by anyone else. He seems to know at once. He sniffs the food like a dog and then if I have not cooked it he will throw the plate away. He has broken so many plates and glasses. Now I use steel plates for him," she told her mother one day, breaking years of silence about her life. "I wish you had made me a bad cook then maybe they would let me be," she whispered stroking her mother's hair as she lay on her death bed. "Feed him, child, feed him all the richness, all the sweetness that he has not given you till the gods see it fit to take him away," her mother said and turned her face to the door to meet the spirit of death who had been waiting for her.

Nanni sang softly, her hands gleaming as she churned the yogurt for the lassi Harish would have for his breakfast. Butter and cream, sugar and khoya, almonds and pistachios – there were so many rich things one could put in a glass of milk. So many wonderful and delicious things that would slowly and gently choke the life out of him. He would not even feel the hands of death gripping him till it was too late and his arteries were clogged with all the sweetness and richness she had poured into his greedy mouth. "I have told you a hundred times not to put whole black pepper into lassi, you bitch can you not hear me? Or have you gone deaf like the rest of your family, the miserable cripples?" he said and threw the glass at her. For the last two days he had been lying in bed with a toothache. One side of his face was swollen. Could the butter and ghee be working their magic already? No, it was too soon. He would die slowly after many years but he would die by her hands, by her cooking. Nanni sliced the almonds finely along with the black pepper in the new glass of lassi which she poured into another tall glass to make it froth. As her bangles tinkled she remembered how he had loved to see her doing this. "You move like a swan rustling its wings. I want to crush you in my arms," he had whispered. His mother was outside supervising the servant as he cleaned the wheat and they had quietly gone up to the attic and made love.

Harish drank the lassi noisily, gulping it down, his throat bobbing like a frog. He had not been always like this. When he was young his eyes were shy and timid and he held her hand on his heart while they slept. Every night she would crush badams in his milk and he would caress her fingers when he drank, not taking his eyes off her face. Even when his mother was in the room, he tried to touch her under the quilt, making her giggle. Now she wished him dead. Every night she saw his body lying on the floor, his thin, unshaven face buried in marigold flowers. When he died she would cry with real grief, her heart would break for the Harish she had known many years ago.

"Butter, fried things, ghee, milk, cream, all banned," he said, slapping his forehead. "The doctor said I have a very high cholestrol and it is all your fault, woman." Harish could eat only boiled food, porridge and dry toast from now on. But that was not possible. "A wife's duty is to cook for her husband," they had told her over and over again for so many years. She must cook his favourite food. He was her husband was he not? She had to look after him or what would people say? Doctors know nothing, just greedy for their fees. "Feed him, feed him all the richness all the sweetness," she could hear her mother singing to her at night. Ghee will make his heart so strong it will burst out of his chest, butter – golden yellow butter she would churn herself – would make his blood so warm and rich that his body would not be able to tolerate its weight. All her cooking skills would now finally be put to test, she would make one rich dish a week to suck the strength out of his veins, one dish to poison his blood, one to clog his veins which run with so much hate for her and her family, I will cook for him one death dish a week, slowly and slowly he will die, not by my hand but because it is the will of the gods. I will look after him like a good wife.

The oil floated on top of the curry as she put the spoon in. She stirred it and then spread a big spoonful on the rice. Then she added a pinch of salt – extra salt was good for him, a bit of ghee and then began mixing the curry and the rice with her hands. Once the proportion was right she made seven equal sized balls and placed them on the steel plate. It was easy for him to eat if she mixed the rice for him. His hands shook a lot these days and he dropped all the food down his clothes. She made gentle cooing sounds as he ate, coaxing him to eat more and sometimes he looked at her with fear and love as if she was his mother. She fed him with her hands because he was too frail to lift the spoon to his mouth. The richer the food, the more she loved feeding him. Each mouthful she gave with her loving hands she hoped would send him closer to his death. "The spirit of death waits for you, I can hear her footsteps down the corridor," she whispered in his ears each night before he fell asleep, his body exhausted by rich greasy curries garnished with burning hot garam masala, sweets floating in cream, fried oily potatoes and a pan filled with coconut, betel nuts, aniseed and thin slivers of dates wrapped in silver foil. The fragrant zarda lulled him to sleep and the lethal curries churned in his stomach to give him nightmares.

Harish slept with his eyes open, his mouth slack as if waiting for more food to be poured into it. He left the room, taking care that Nanni could not see him floating out of the window into the sky. He loved her still but when she sat before him, her breasts soft against his arms his body shook with a terrible desire which frightened him. Her gaping mouth looked at him as if she wanted to devour him like a witch he had once seen hiding in the forest many summers ago. The woman had stood still watching him and then touched his face with her long fingers. He ran home, crying silently all the way and when he looked at his face in the mirror, there were blue scars where she had touched him though he had felt no pain. Nanni was a gentle girl once and her eyes looked upon him with love. Then slowly she began to grow. At first her eyes grew large and then her hands reached to the floor. He had to control her by shouting and beating her or else she would kill him once day. Her breasts were huge now, almost as big as her body. When she sat next to him feeding him like a good wife should, he could not breathe. He tried to push her away but each day his arms grew weaker and weaker. She sucked all the strength out with each mouthful she thrust in his mouth with her long, soft fingers. He had to fly away each night from her terrible power, to look for a safer place where she could not follow him, where she could not feed him with her long witch's fingers. He could hear whispers at night and even when he shut his ears and crawled under the bed, the voices followed him. Nanni spoke to him so gently when he was awake but at night she was the witch who would scar his face with her white nails. He wanted to shout at her, grab her neck and shake her like he used to when his mother was alive to protect him, but his body would not obey. He lay like an animal who had given up hope, swollen and white and the witch's hands made blue marks all over his body. Nanni's face, her glinting eyes grew bigger when he tried to lift his head to look at her. He had to push her away but his speech slurred when he tried to shout at her. If only he could catch hold of her once, break her into pieces, he would be safe. But she towered above him now, weighing him down with her breasts. But she would not harm him. She was a good wife and it was her duty to look after him, to feed him till his dying day.